I0658054

The Guy in the Box

A Short Story Collection

IAIN S. BAIRD

Published by:
Southern Yellow Pine (SYP) Publishing
4351 Natural Bridge Rd.
Tallahassee, FL 32305

www.syppublishing.com

This is a work of fiction. Names, characters, places, and events that occur either are the products of the author's imagination or are used fictitiously. Any resemblance to actual persons, places, or events is purely coincidental.

The contents and opinions expressed in this book do not necessarily reflect the views and opinions of Southern Yellow Pine Publishing, nor does the mention of brands or trade names constitute endorsement.

ISBN-10: 1-59616-072-1
ISBN-13: 978-1-59616-072-9
ISBN-13: ePub 978-1-59616-073-6
ISBN-13: Adobe PDF eBook 978-1-59616-074-3
Library of Congress Control Number: 2018952223

Printed in the United States of America
First Edition
July 2018

Dedication

For my children, Sara and Michael

Praise for the Author

Iain Baird's story collection, *The Guy in the Box*, promises to intellectually engage and delight readers as he explores the human condition with both humor and insight. Those who discovered Baird's memoir, *Two Storms*, will know they are once again in the hands of a master story teller.

Laura Oliver, author of *The Story Within.* (Penguin Random House) Award winning author of essay and fiction and Creative Writing Instructor, St. Johns College, MD.

In these remarkable tales, Iain Baird lets his fertile imagination run loose over the globe from the Bronx to New Delhi, from the redwoods to Paris in a rainbow of character study and plot twists that we follow, mouth open, in willing suspension of disbelief.

We trail behind Baird's inventions as adolescent mischief morphs into unintended arson and the death of a despised teacher. We watch an aging couple make a final run for independence on a road trip into Mexico. We discover a secret half-sister in India is not a blood sister after all, but a soul sister. A man in late-stage dementia, attending the funeral of a friend, stuns us and the mourners around him, asking "Who's in the box?" A cab fare in New York City is paid with memories of the Khyber Pass. Two boys, would-be fur traders, trap a muskrat on the banks of the Bronx River. And we're off to Paris where an accidental tourist sits at a cafe table about to be struck by a veering car.

A wide circle of literary magazines has already recognized the unhurried, elegant style of Iain Baird. He deserves a far wider public.

John Rolfe Gardiner, author of *Newport Rising*

Contents

The Flight

The old man dreamt about flying. Not the dream where he sprung from the high-board in a perfect swan dive and sailed out beyond the pool to sweep down, skimming his fingers across the swells of Tampa Bay, before gaining height once again over Ybor City and returning to flip mid-air, slicing through the pool's glassy, blue surface with barely a ripple. And it wasn't the white-knuckled, scream-yourself-awake nightmare of being in the flaming 747-jetliner tumbling toward the spinning earth. No, this was the helicopter dream—his favorite. He was young, once again flying solo over the frozen hills near Taegu. Choppers were new to combat in Korea, and the brass wasn't quite sure what to make of them. But he knew. They were the future. He was conducting aerial observation missions for the artillery, but he could see the day when the helicopter would replace the truck in moving around troops and supplies, just as the truck had replaced the horse. In his dream, he was forty. Virile, sharp, and striking in his colonel's flight suit. In command. He was banking the helicopter to the right when he heard the warning bell. He checked his gauges but couldn't see any flashing lights. The bell chimed again.

He struggled up from sleep. Pain surged through his flaring joints. He was ninety-three years old, living in Oxford Towers, in Tampa, Florida. He was still in his own apartment though his children were scheming to shift him over to the assisted living wing. He was lying on a rubber sheet. He took a deep breath and sighed as he opened his eyes. He had no idea what time it was though daylight streamed through the window as he squinted against the glare. He thought it might be Thursday, but he wouldn't take a bet on it. He heard the bell, yet again. It was his phone.

"Dad? Dad?"

"Huh? What?"

"Dad, is that you?"

"Who?"

"Dad. It's Mary."

"Mary? Oh, Mary. Yeah."

"You okay? You got your hearing aid in?"

"What? No, wait a minute." He swung his tortured legs over the side of the bed and sat up. His head spun, and he thought he might faint back on to the bed, but his head cleared, and he reached over to the nightstand and lifted his glasses to his face. He slipped the hearing aids into his scaly ears.

"Dad? You okay?"

"Sure, I'm okay." He looked down at his spindly, chalky legs ending in the swollen purple ankles. He raised his eyes to the white walls covered in plaques and commendations. One dusty frame held a tilted display of his service ribbons. His scarred desk was piled high with newspaper clippings and unopened envelopes.

"Dad, you sound a little disoriented."

"Well, I was taking a nap."

"At ten in the morning?"

He squinted at the clock sitting next to the row of pills on his wooden night table. "At my age, I can take a nap whenever I damn well feel like it," he said. "It was only for a few minutes."

"So, you're up?"

"Of course, I'm up. Dressed, showered, shaved, the whole nine yards," he said, running a hand across his two-day stubble, and he had to piss something awful. "Look, I gotta run. I promised Betty I'd drive her over to the base. She needs to get some stuff from the commissary."

"Why don't you take a taxi? You don't need to drive. Wouldn't that be easier?"

"Look, I gotta run."

"Be careful. I'll call tomorrow."

He reached for his cane and started seesawing back and forth. When he had momentum, he squatted forward and, grasping the cane with both hands, groaned to a standing position. He shuffled into the bathroom and dropped the soggy diaper to his ankles and stepped out of it. He pointed his penis with his right hand and used his left to steady himself against the wall. *Used to be able to piss like a horse.* Now, it was as if his dick had a stutter, sputtering dark yellow urine all over the bowl. He shook off the last drops, lowered the seat, and sat down, holding on to the handrail for support.

He sat for a moment staring at the towel rack while he caught his breath. The bright fluorescent light hummed overhead. With his cane, he snared the yellowed diaper and tipped it into the trashcan. He reached over and got a fresh one out of the carton under the sink. He stepped into the plastic, padded underpants and pulled them up to his knees. Now came the hard part— holding on to the diaper so it didn't drop to the floor. While placing his other hand on the rail to pull himself erect, he wrestled the pants up and over his bony hips. At one time, he'd been a swimmer for the University of Florida, known for his graceful dives and explosive bursts of speed in the one hundred meters. Now, it took him an hour to get dressed.

The dining room at Oxford Towers featured silverware, white tablecloths, waiters in dark trousers, white shirts, and black bow ties; and the room itself overlooked the bay. Today, he was lunching with Betty Rodriguez.

Betty wasn't much to look at, probably never had been. She had a smile of jagged, yellow teeth that would spook a pterodactyl. But she always wore flashy, floral dresses and thick braids of gold around her neck. She was short and squat, but she had good legs, accented by the four-inch high heels she always wore. She had a passion for life and a recklessness he found intoxicating. She said what she thought, did what she wanted, and seemed to get away with it all. Being rich probably didn't hurt, but he suspected she'd been single-minded long before she married the oil baron down in Mexico in the Thirties. Long widowed, she now let her children and grandchildren run the family businesses, but Betty was careful to keep a controlling interest in the holding company that had made them all rich. The old man wasn't impressed with her money. He'd made plenty of his own in real estate over the years, but he did admire her balls. Bigger balls than most of the men he knew.

"That woman of yours coming in today?" Betty asked.

"What?" he asked, looking up from his menu.

"That colored woman of yours. Charlene. Charlene coming in today?"

"Oh. No. She doesn't come till tomorrow."

"Well, when she comes, you tell her you need clean clothes. You gonna sit with me, you gotta look the part. Okay?"

"Okay," he said, taking a drink of water and straightening the napkin on his lap. "Say, we going to the base later? I need to go by the credit union and get some cash. I'm supposed to pay Charlene on Fridays."

"You up to driving?"

4

"Of course, I'm up to driving." Everyone seemed to know about his driving problems. Three months ago, he'd sideswiped an empty Ford truck on the way to his doctor's appointment. When the doctor realized he'd had another accident, he'd sent off some paperwork to the DMV, and the DMV sent a letter telling him they were going to revoke his license based on medical reasons. He fought it, of course, hiring a high-priced lawyer to make the bureaucrats at the DMV snap to attention. He got a new medical evaluation from a friendly doctor and a reprieve, though it involved a new driving test. Fortunately, his driving record was clean. Though he'd had a number of fender benders recently, he found that a handful of cash precluded the involvement of the police and the insurance companies. He always carried lots of cash.

At the DMV, he'd passed the eye test though he was blind in one eye from a botched cataract operation twenty years earlier. Seemed there was no law in Florida against one-eyed drivers. He'd squeaked through the written test, taking more than an hour on the ten-minute exam. Then, there was the road test.

"What will you have for lunch, today, sir?"

"Oh." He looked at the menu again. "I'll have the Salisbury steak and mashed potatoes and carrots. And let me have a bowl of that beef barley soup." He'd taken to having his big meal at lunch. Then he could just heat up some oatmeal or scramble a couple of eggs for dinner in his apartment. By the end of the day, he was bushed.

"So, you still got your license? I don't want to drive around with a felon," said Betty, chomping into a roll smeared with butter.

"Yeah, I can still drive, but I have to take the road test again." He was so sure he'd passed it. He'd followed the directions of the examiner to the letter. But instead of half an hour, the test had only taken five minutes.

"Well, that was easy," he'd said at the time.

"Sir, I don't think you understand. You failed."

"Failed? How could I have failed? I did exactly what you told me."

"Well, you blew through the first stop sign, then you turned left through another stop sign, and then turned right through the next one without stopping at either. You only get three mistakes."

"But you never told me to stop. You said go straight, go left, go right. I did it exactly as you said."

"Yeah, but it's a stop sign. You're supposed to stop. It's a driving test, after all."

He'd raised Cain, telling the DMV people how he'd fought in two wars, how he'd flown helicopters before they were even born, but they wouldn't relent. They gave him a driving permit, just like some snot-nosed teenager, and told him to come back for a retest in sixty days. He couldn't drive unless accompanied by an adult driver. Well, Betty was an adult and still had her license, though she hadn't actually driven in thirty years.

"You going to ask me how my doctor's appointment went?" asked Betty.

"What? Oh. No. Old people sitting around talking about their doctors' appointments. I hate that."

"I know, and that's why I like hanging out with you. You don't complain too much, not like most of these old geezers, but this is a bit different. I need your help, but you have to understand the whole picture."

"Okay. I got time." He smiled. It was one of their jokes. Time—so little of it, so much of it. So few long, long days.

6

"Well, the doctor says I've got an aneurysm," Betty said, pointing to the right side of her head. "A balloon in my brain. Problem is it could pop at any minute. Bang, I'm dead."

"Jesus, Betty."

"Yeah, ain't that a kick in the ass?"

He frowned a bit, not only at the news but at her swearing.

"Can't they do anything?"

"Sure. They can cut off the top of my head and put a patch on it. But with my heart, the doctor says the operation would kill me. So, either way I'm a dead duck."

"Jeez, how—"

"How long? Who knows? They won't even make a guess, though it could be any minute. Even before we have coffee if that girl doesn't hurry up. Say sweetheart," Betty yelled across the room, "two black coffees."

"I don't know what to say, Betty. I'm sorry." And he was. Betty was one of the few people he still enjoyed.

"Kick in the ass."

This time he didn't frown.

"Anyway, the doctor said my dizzy spells might get worse. My kids want to put me in the assisted living center."

"Oh, Betty, don't do that. My kids want me there, too. They don't think I can take care of myself any longer. They think I'm shell-shocked or something but don't go there. It's a bad place." They'd put Patti there, his wife of sixty-four years. Trouble breathing one night. Next thing she was in the hospital. Next thing dead. Now his kids wanted to put him there. His son lived over near Orlando, but his daughters were out of state—one in Maryland, the other in Michigan. At one time, soon after Patti died, he suggested he move in with one of them, but there'd been no takers. Truth was they got on his nerves probably about the same as he got on theirs. Though they only visited him once every

7

few months, somehow, they thought they knew what was best for him. They didn't want the responsibility of caring for him, but they didn't want the guilt either. Just put him away. That seemed to be their solution. Well, screw them. He wasn't going anywhere. He was still the parent. They were the children. They should be supportive, obedient. Instead, they went around behind his back and tried to undermine him. Tried to get him shipped over to the sick bay. Tried to take his car away from him. Tried to destroy him. Screw them. He'd do what he wanted. He always had.

He looked over at Betty. "Don't go into the assisted living unit. Don't do it."

"Hell, I'm not going there. I got other plans."

"Oh?"

"Mexico. I'm going to Mexico. I want to see the house I lived in when I first got married, when I was a young bride. I want to breathe the warm air and look out at the Eastern Sierra Madre Mountains. I haven't been there in almost seventy years. We only lived in Mexico two years before heading north, but those were the two most wonderful years of my life. I want to see my first home."

"Mexico. That's a long flight." He avoided complaining about flying. Betty had heard it all before. How they degraded you by making you take off your shoes. How they made you open your belt buckle. Young black kids in sloppy uniforms waving those beeping wands at him, poking him. The stewardess telling him he'd have to calm down or they'd remove him from the plane. He—a veteran of two wars. A pilot. He'd written to the President asking for a special pass, but they'd blown him off with a form letter.

"I won't be flying," she said. "The aneurysm. The change in cabin pressure is too risky. I've been grounded."

"Then how will you get to Mexico?"

She smiled her jagged grin at him and batted her mascara-laden eyes. "You changed the oil in that big, old, white Caddy of yours recently?"

It was pretty much a straight shot. Interstate 75 out of Tampa up to I-10. Then I-10 west for about one thousand miles to San Antonio. Then 150 miles to the border at Laredo. Betty was a wiz on the computer and had gotten detailed directions off something called MapQuest. The Mexican portion to Monterrey might be a bit dicey. The old man had no confidence in the Mexican road system though the map said they would be on the Pan American Highway most of the way.

They agreed to drive 250 to 300 miles each day—five or six hours. They planned to get on the road early in the morning when the sun would be behind them and not bouncing off the windshield. Neither could sleep much past six anyway. They'd stop for breakfast halfway. By then, his knees would be screaming, and he'd stagger about the parking lot trying to loosen his joints. At lunchtime, they'd stop again, exhausted, and find a motel. Naps were important. They made Tallahassee the first night. At this rate, the whole trip should take a week, surely no more than ten days.

In Tallahassee, Betty had suggested they share a room—two double beds to conserve their cash, but he'd demurred. He thought they had enough money. Between them, they'd withdrawn almost ten thousand dollars before hitting the road. He didn't want to use any credit cards, at least until they hit Mexico. He suspected their kids would be trying to find them soon enough to put an end to the trip. Besides, sharing a room wouldn't be proper. He'd not shared a bedroom with another woman besides Patti since they were married, except for those few Korean women during the war, but that didn't really count.

In the motel room, he turned on the television and flipped through the channels. He watched a music show for a minute with his mouth open, a bunch of kids in large shirts with rings through their faces yelling and screaming. He turned off the set. He didn't watch much TV. Sure, he'd catch the Gators' football games when they were on, but aside from that, he only watched the evening news, which always pissed him off, and Lawrence Welk reruns, which always calmed him down. He used to joke to Patti that Lawrence Welk sure could direct a band, especially for a dead guy. Welk played his kind of music, and sometimes he and Patti would get up and take a spin around the living room when one of their favorite tunes came on.

As a young man at the University of Florida, he'd been quite the dancer. He and his fraternity brothers from ATO would cross over the county line and go dancing at a juke joint down in Ocala. He'd drape a wet washcloth around his neck to absorb the sweat and to keep him cool as he jitterbugged to the swing music. He'd jump and jive his way across the sawdust covered floor, the strings of colored lights blurring as he spun around as if he were caught in the center of an out-of-control carousel. As he turned faster and faster, the music would blare louder and louder, bouncing off walls, ceiling, and floor, to the point that it seemed to be coming from within him. In those moments, he'd felt as if his feet were no longer earthbound, as if he were flying. When his dancing partner removed the damp cloth from his neck to mop her brow, he knew that they'd soon be sipping rum and coke and smooching in the backseat of his '31 DeSoto. Yeah, he liked Lawrence Welk, even if it was on that leftist, liberal PBS television station.

He turned away from the television and lay across the motel's bed, fully dressed. He was thinking about taking off his shoes when he fell asleep.

Two mornings later, they stopped at the Huddle House outside of Lafayette, Louisiana.

"What do you want for breakfast?" Betty asked.

"Huh? Oh. The cheese omelet."

"You had that yesterday morning."

"Yeah, but they make them good. Really fluffy. Just like I like them."

He looked out the window just as a police cruiser pulled in beside his Cadillac. The officer got out of his car, but instead of coming into the restaurant, he circled the Caddy, paying special attention to the license plate.

"Uh oh," the old man said, grasping the edge of the booth's table and easing himself to his feet. He grabbed his cane and shuffled out to the parking lot, the cop turning toward him as he approached.

"This your car?"

"Yep."

"Can I see your license?"

As he pulled the wallet out of his back pocket, Betty joined him.

"What's going on?" she asked.

The police officer looked at his permit. "You ninety-three?"

"I know I don't look it."

"Sir, this is a driving permit."

"What?"

"A driving permit."

"Oh. Yeah. But it's legal. I'm with an adult driver."

Betty leaned forward, flashing her best reptilian grin.

11

"I'm afraid it's only legal in Florida. It's no good out of state. Certainly not in Louisiana."

"Where does it say that?"

"Right here in capital letters across the face of the permit. Valid only in the State of Florida. See?"

As the old man squinted at the permit, the walkie-talkie on the officer's shoulder barked, "A 211 in progress at the EZ Mart on Maple. Code 3. 10-0."

"Damn," the cop said, handing the permit back to him. "Here. Don't drive anymore. Let the lady drive. And call your children."

As the cop sped off with lights flashing and siren blaring, he and Betty looked at each other. Call your children? The word was out.

When they checked in at the motel in San Antonio, he asked for a ground floor, handicapped room as usual. The only concessions they made to the disabled at these places were the handrails in the shower and those next to the high-riser toilet, but they were enough. The road trip must be good for him. He was feeling spryer. This morning he was even up for a shower though it took him several minutes to figure out the pull/push faucet and to get the hot/cold ratio of the water just right. After pulling on a fresh diaper, he put on clean clothes for the first time on the trip. He wondered where he would get the soiled clothes washed. Then he thought to hell with it and threw them into the trash. He'd treat himself to a new shirt and pair of pants when they got to Mexico. Mexico. Maybe they could make the border today. If not, certainly by tomorrow. There really wasn't any hurry.

They'd be getting a late start today. Last night, they'd sat up watching a movie, *The Treasure of Sierra Madre* with Humphrey Bogart. Somehow it seemed appropriate, being about Mexico and all. They argued a bit about dinner. She wanted to order in Chinese food, but he hated that slimy stuff and referred to it as Chinky food, and then he had to hear a lecture from Betty about him being prejudiced. He suggested cheeseburgers, but she said she didn't like to eat too much beef. They settled on pizza but not before arguing some more over the toppings. He wanted pepperoni, she veggie. They ordered half and half so everyone was happy though Betty didn't eat much of hers anyway. The last thing he remembered was some Mexican in a sombrero saying he didn't need no stinky badges or something and Betty snoring softly on the other bed. When he woke in the morning, Betty had gone back to her room.

By the time they got on the road, it was close to ten. They grabbed some juice and donuts in the motel lobby just as the staff was closing down the complimentary breakfast. They took travel cups of coffee for the road.

The old man turned on the radio. When it played "South of the Border, Down Mexico Way," he smiled. Mexico. They were really going to make it. Due to the late start, it was well after two when he suggested they stop for a late lunch before making the final push on to the border.

"There's a turn-off up ahead. They've got a Huddle House. Might be the last chance for a cheese omelet."

When she didn't answer, he squinted over at her. Her eyes were closed, her chin rested on her chest, a faint smile graced her lips. Her breath was still.

"Betty?"

He reached over and shook her shoulder. Her head slipped to the right. He pulled over to the side of the road. Looking at her quiet face, he reached over and took her still hand in his. He thought of Patti and of all the other losses over the years. There was such little left. And he thought of his children and the assisted living unit and all they had planned for him. They thought he was losing his mind. But Betty had understood; he wasn't crazy; he was just old. This trip probably sent them over the edge. That cop showing up in Lafayette meant the authorities were now involved. His kids were hot on his trail. Probably had some kind of order to commit him either to the loony bin or the sick bay. It didn't matter which. His days of freedom were numbered.

He sipped some cold coffee and looked at Betty and thought of his mission to get her to Mexico. He'd said he'd take her there. She wouldn't care now, but still. And Mexico. He hadn't thought much about it, but maybe he could get a place there. Maybe Monterrey or down by the sea in Vera Cruz. Maybe his kids couldn't reach him there. With all his money, he could probably set himself up in style, provided they hadn't frozen his accounts or something. He drove on to a Seven-Eleven and bought some fresh coffee and rations for the rest of the trip, snicker-snacks he called them: Snickers, Three Musketeers, Doritos, and a half dozen glazed donuts. He also paid for some Extra Strength Tylenol to help him make it the rest of the way.

The old man knew he shouldn't be driving at night. He could still drive fine in the daytime, regardless of what everyone said, but nighttime was different, yet he was so close to the border, he pressed on. He squinted his good eye and tilted his head to the side so that he could get a better view of the dim road before him. It was the glare of the oncoming lights he found most difficult to see around.

He slowed down as he approached the crossing at Laredo. Betty sat on the seat beside him, secured by the seat belt fastened tightly around her. He could see the bridge across the Rio Grande lit up ahead of him. As he approached, a U.S. border official

14

raised a hand signaling him to stop. The guard walked around the car shining a flashlight on the Caddy's license plate while speaking into his walkie-talkie. The guard approached the car, winding his hand around, indicating the old man should lower his window. The guard shined the light in his face and then over at Betty.

"What's going on?"

"Huh?"

"I said, 'What's going on?'"

"Oh. Nothing. But keep your voice down. She's sleeping." He put his finger to his lips and nodded toward Betty propped up stiff as a board on the Cadillac's passenger seat.

"Sleeping? Pull over to the side there, sir." The guard waved the beam from his light toward a parking space at the side of the road next to a booth.

"But—"

"Now, sir."

The old man took a deep breath and exhaled, looking ahead at the bridge, Mexico, there on the other side, so close. He glanced once at Betty, then slipped the Cadillac into gear and floored the accelerator. He heard a scraping sound, and the car shook as he sideswiped a concrete barrier. But then he was on the bridge. He sped up as he approached the Mexican side. Floodlights came on blinding him in their glare, but he kept going. He could just make out a series of booths, sort of like checkpoints, and he pointed the Caddy between two of them. Soldiers in green uniforms were waving, and a bar descended in the gateway before him. The bar exploded across the windshield as he sped through. Mexico. He was in Mexico. Maybe they'd give him political asylum, he thought, as he lost control of the car and it vaulted over an embankment.

The flight seemed to last forever. Through the dark, he thought he could make out the hills of Taegu. The rotors were thumping, and they comforted him. He eased the throttle to the right to steady the chopper and to raise the nose, which seemed to be drifting downward.

He thought of his young wife waiting for his return from war and the small baby back home whom he had yet to hold in his arms. He adjusted the attitude of the joystick to correct the tilt to the left, his hand steady, his legs strong, working the rudder pedals. His vision was clear as he aimed the chopper at the horizon and flew on into the night.

The Guildemeister

Ronny Jefferson's most prized possession is the carved walnut walking stick with the solid gold handle, the shape and size of a cue ball. Well, maybe his second most valuable possession, if you consider the pair of artificial legs given to him by the V.A. after his discharge from the Army in '73. But neither the legs nor cane are with him now in Washington, DC. They wait for him in a closet in the rear of a one-bedroom apartment off a vine-covered courtyard on Dumaine Street in the French Quarter. It'll be two weeks more until Ronny is back in New Orleans.

In the meantime, this morning finds Ronny dragging himself up Washington's Thirteenth Street toward the corner of F where he'll set up shop for the day. He rolls his legless body on his homemade dolly to the northwest corner, all the better to catch the morning sunshine. He sets down his harmonium and an upturned, battered fedora and begins to play the blues. He never begs, nevertheless, every hour or so, he'll have to empty the hat of the crumpled dollar bills and loose change to make room for more. Sometimes, he sings along with his playing.

"My baby done left me cause I's three feet tall,
Says I just too short to consider to ball.
Say she want a big man in every way,
I'd have to grow a foot or two to make her stay.

Blues? I gots the short man blues.
Blues? Gots nothing more to lose.

"Ronny, you nasty." That's Baby speaking.

Baby's a receptionist who works at a Think Tank up on K Street and who always dresses a lot better than one should be able to afford on a receptionist's salary, even a receptionist on K Street.

"Baby, Baby. You lookin' fine today," he says. "When you gonna give ole Ronny a tumble?"

"I told you, you ain't my type."

"What? You don't like black men?"

"I don't like musicians."

"Well, you ever change your mind, you know where to find me."

With a smile, Baby drops a dollar in Ronny's hat and sashays up the street. Ronny watches her for a moment. Elegant. He sighs and rolls his dolly a bit to the left, following the sun's rays.

And so the day goes. A dollar here, a handful of change there. At ten, the bald, white dude, who works at one of the federal agencies, drops off the cup of Starbucks—tall, double-shot, skim latte. At twelve-fifteen, the shoe store guy with the marital problems on his way to the tittie bar on Ninth sets down a bag lunch. After taking a break to eat the ham and cheese sandwich, Ronny hefts the harmonium up on to his dolly and wheels himself across the street to stay in the warmth of the sun.

I'd walk a mile on hot coals if I only had feet,
I'd crawl right up your driveway if I wasn't so damn beat,
I'd climb the highest mountain, I would swim the deepest sea,
But you can see without no legs, that just ain't goin' to be.

Blues? I gots the short man blues.
Blues? Gots nothing more to lose.

A cool breeze stirs the dollars in Ronny's hat. He looks up to the sky and sees the sun skimming the edge of the building across the way. Soon he'll be in shadow. Johnny Puke saunters up the street toward him. Puke ain't his real name, of course, but it's how Ronny thinks of him. He's called Johnny Pucker up on Fourteenth Street near Thomas Circle where he runs his whores; probably not his real name neither. Johnny drops a fin into the hat.

"Why thank you, Mr. Pucker. Very generous."

"You got your ear out for me?"

"Always, Mr. Pucker."

"You hear anything I should know, you going to apprise me, right?"

"Right," Ronny calls after him as Johnny continues his pimp roll up the street.

'Yeah, right, Mr. Puke," he mutters to himself.

The wind blows again, this time even cooler. The season's ending. Ronny packs up the harmonium, takes the last fistful of dollars from the hat, which he places on his head, and sets off back down Thirteenth Street. He grunts softly as he pulls his trolley along the pavement with his two muscular arms, inching along like a two-legged caterpillar.

Even before the Southwest flight touches down at Louis Armstrong Airport in New Orleans, the annual metamorphosis of Ronny has begun. Gone are the shabby clothes, replaced now by a well-tailored, blue blazer and a pink shirt tied at the neck with a golden tie. The dolly is left behind in DC. In its stead is a wheel chair with a black leather seat and a chrome finish, which in turn will soon be set aside. In place of the battered fedora, Ronny sports a jaunty bowler made from gold silk, which he tips to the pretty ladies as he rolls past.

With minimal assistance from the airport cabby, Ronny exits the taxi and gets into his wheel chair in front of the French Quarter building on Dumaine, and with his one piece of hand luggage on his lap, he rolls himself under the wrought iron balcony, past the massive carriageway doors, and into the courtyard. There, he inserts the old skeleton key into the lock of his apartment. The Guildemeister is home.

The whole thing had started with the shoes. He'd just been Ronny Jefferson on that day some ten years ago on a visit to New Orleans to see his sister, a sometimes-jazz singer on Frenchmen Street. He'd strapped on his legs and was taking a stroll up Magazine Street looking for a place to grab a beer and an oyster Po' Boy when he saw the shoes in the window of Bertha's Vintage Emporium, shiny gold shoes that looked like they just might slip right on to his prostheses. And damned if they didn't. He thought how nicely they'd go with the gold-handled walking stick presented to him by the members of his platoon as a talisman of hope after the Bouncing Betty took both his legs in the Delta north of Can Tho. The golden bowler and tie soon followed. The 24-karat grillwork for his teeth were a later addition, a year or two after he'd already been baptized at Sonny's Bar one night in a river of Abita beer.

"Who you trying to be, Ronny?" asked Crab Man, named for the spasmodic, sideways manner in which he danced after a few drinks. "What's with the shoes and shit?"

"He trying to be that guy from the Bond movie. Goldfucker or something," said Renée, draped across the bar, only a nod or two from oblivion.

"Just trying to add a little class to the joint," said Ronny tipping his gold bowler.

"You Gold, Ronny. Solid Gold," said Crab Man, trying to stay on Ronny's good side, seeing that he was doing the buying.

"Ya, you ist de Guildemeister, all right," added some tourist from Holland, decked out in shorts and walking shoes. He'd made a left when he should've made a right and ended up in Sonny's Bar on the wrong side of Rampart Street, too drunk to notice that he was the only white guy in the place. The Guildemeister, or at least that was the consensus on what the Dutch guy had said when everyone sobered up a bit the next day. The Guildemeister. Yeah, that would do.

And so it comes to pass that every fall when the breezes grew nippy up north, Ronny Jefferson wheels himself down Thirteenth Street in DC for the last time and emerges a couple of days later from his French Quarter apartment with his legs strapped on, sporting the gold shoes, tie, and bowler, swinging the gold-handled walking stick, and flashing his 24-karat smile. In April or May, when the air in New Orleans grows sultry, the Guildemeister disappears and the Blues singing, harmonium playing destitute takes up his position behind his upturned fedora on the corner of Thirteenth and F Streets in DC.

It's a good living. During the summer months in Washington, Ronny takes in a surprising thirty to forty thousand dollars. It's amazing how those dollars in the fedora add up, hour after hour, day after day, week after week. And overhead? What overhead? Adds up enough to support the Guildemeister's wintering in New Orleans, that's for sure. Wintering in New Orleans. How he loves the sound of that. Reminds him of the rich white folks who winter in Miami and summer in the Hamptons.

Around New Orleans, he cuts quite the figure, and this in a city known for its figure cutting. Either strolling down Royal

Street on Sunday mornings, admiring the window displays of Louis Quatorze chairs and cracked Dalton china and listening to the street musicians, or stumbling up Bourbon Street at four in the morning, trading quips with the hookers looking for a last John, one and all hail the Guildemeister. His notoriety grows to such an extent that two years ago, he sat on a throne in a mule drawn cart to lead the Krewe du Vieux parade as it opened the Mardi Gras season, wending its way through the narrow streets of the Quarter. For that occasion, he'd donned a shiny gold lamé suit and cape to complement his other golden accessories. He looked like the Sun King himself as he waved to his screaming, sloshed subjects along the parade route. The suit and cape now hang, cleaned and pressed, in his closet. One day he plans to be buried in them.

Yes, it's all pretty sweet. Six months sitting in the sun in DC, singing and smiling and watching his hat fill with dollars then six months drinking and partying in the Big Easy. Oh yeah, there's partying. The Guildemeister strikes quite the figure decked out in gold, but that's not all; he's also an oddity. A man with no legs. How would that work? And New Orleans seems to attract just the kind of women determined to find out. Yep, pretty sweet, all things considering. Pretty sweet, until Baby shows up.

"I know you."

"Huh?" the Guildemeister says, looking up from his beer.

"I know you. You Ronny. You that legless guy up on F Street."

"I think you're mistaken," says the Guildemeister, flashing his golden grillwork and standing up from the table. "I think you've mistaken me for someone else, Miss."

"What the fuck," says Baby, looking up at the tall man standing in front of her. "Jesus, you know you got a double up in DC."

22

It might have ended there, a few more polite words, and she would have been her on way, if at that exact moment the Crab Man hadn't shown up.

"Ronny, my man, you ain't goin'o believe the shit that went down today. Whoa, who's this fine lady? Ain't you goin' to introduce me to your friend, Ronny?"

"It is you," says Baby. "What the fuck is going on? Where'd you get them legs? Shit, if you ain't the sight."

Ronny, or the Guildemeister—frankly, he doesn't know who he is at the moment—grabs Baby by the elbow and steers her over to a corner table away from the prying eyes and cupped ears that lined the bar.

"Where'd you get them legs?" Baby asks.

"Nam."

"What you mean 'Nam'? Like Namin Marcus, the department store?"

"Neiman Marcus. No, 'Nam', like Vietnam."

"Before my time."

"I guess."

"What was you doing there?" Baby asks, checking out the Guildemeister from head to toe and back up again.

Ronny looks across the room. "I don't talk about it." He never talks about his days as a sniper, blowing the heads off VC big shots from five hundred yards out—the pop of his rifle followed a second later by the head vaporizing into a red mist that sprayed the surrounding jungle. He never talks about how he climbed down one evening from his perch in a banyan tree to step on the mine buried in the rotted leaves and tangled vines below.

"Let's get out of here," the Guildemeister says, pulling a thick roll of greenbacks out of his pocket and dropping a twenty on the table.

Baby's eyes widen at the sight of the wad of bills, and she looks left and right. "Jesus, Ronny, ain't you ever heard of a bank. Don't you got a credit card?'

"No credit cards, no check books, no banks. Don't trust 'em."

"Well, I got a Platinum American Express card."

"Ain't that nice."

Ronny wakes to the sound of an engine slamming into a line of freight cars. He hears the train sound its whistle as it reverses direction to begin the long haul north carrying coffee or steel or one of the other hundreds of commodities unloaded at the Port of New Orleans. Out on the river, a tanker sounds its foghorn. Ronny looks at the clock. Three twenty. He rolls over, wondering if Baby might be ready to go again. He has a few other legless tricks to show her. But Baby's gone. He raises his head and looks toward the bathroom. Dark. Damn, she has gone. Maybe he's losing his touch. Maybe she'll come back. Baby's special. Elegant. And talented. The Guildemeister smiles with the memory of just how talented Baby can be.

Bracing himself on the night table and the arm of his wheel chair, he swings himself onto the seat and rolls across the room to the toilet. When he reenters the bedroom, the first thing he notices is that one of his legs has fallen to the floor and is no longer propped up next to the chair where he left it. Then he sees his trousers lying crumpled in the corner. Shit. He shakes his head as he searches each pocket, knowing already the money's gone. More than two thousand dollars. As he tilts his head to the right, considering if she had been worth it, he notices the closet door ajar. The closet where he keeps the rest of his stash.

He sits looking out at the night sky. All his money gone. Thirty-eight thousand dollars. He thinks about heading back up to DC, putting his hat out again, but it's winter, and he hates the cold. In the cold, his whole body aches, even the phantom legs that have been gone so long. He wheels around back into the room just in time to see his door explode inward, and there in its frame stands Johnny Puke.

"Where's the Bitch?"

"Who—"

The blow catches Ronny by surprise high on the left cheek, and his chair spins around.

He never expected it. Who'd hit a cripple?

"Don't play stupid with me? Baby. The Bitch. Where is she?"

"Baby? What Baby got to do with you?"

This time Ronny raises his hand in time to deflect the blow, pain jolting down his left arm.

"Don't fuck with me, you legless creep. Where's Baby?"

"She's gone. Robbed me. Took all my money."

The wind seems to sail right out of Johnny Puke. He takes a deep breath and sits on the edge of the bed. "She rob you, too, huh?"

Things fall into place for Ronny. "Baby. She work for you?"

"Of course she work for me. How'd you think she get all them fancy clothes and jewelry and shit, by answering the phone up on K Street? So, where's Baby? Where'd she go?"

"I don't know," says Ronny, still dazed by the blow to the head and the onslaught of these new developments.

"You don't know. Well, I know one thing. I'm going to find her, and you're going to help," says Johnny Puke, rising to his feet.

The next evening in Sonny's, the Guildemeister addresses the League of Lushes. "You all remember that girl who came in here last night.

"Yeah, the one who knew you from somewhere. 'F'in Street or something. What was that all about?" asks the Crab Man.

"Was I here last night?" asks Renée, lifting her head, widening her eyes, and blinking around the room.

Sonny pours the Guildemeister a shot and rests his massive forearms on the counter.

"Forget that F Street stuff. Anyway, I need to find the girl."

Everyone resumes their drinking, except Sonny, who takes his soiled dishrag farther down the bar and wipes at a decade-old stain.

"Her name's Baby," says the Guildemeister. Still nothing. "I got a thousand dollars."

The Crab Man's eyes pop open, and Renée looks like someone has hit her with a defibrillator—full voltage.

"Huh?" asks Sonny, saying something for the first time in weeks besides 'What'll it be?'

And so the search begins. Ronny and his cohorts put out the word through their connections in every dive and flop house in New Orleans. Meanwhile, Johnny Puke hits the cribs and sends out the call through the International Brotherhood of Pimps and Perverts.

With every other person in the French Quarter combing the alleys and hidden courtyards, who would think it would be Renée on a visit to her sister in Uptown who'd spot Baby getting off a streetcar and crossing St. Charles Avenue to enter the fashionable Lafitte Bed and Breakfast.

An hour later, when Johnny Puke and the Guildemeister enter her room, Baby's conveniently counting the money on the brocade bedspread of the canopy bed.

"Here, Baby, let me give you a hand with that," says Johnny Puke.

Baby looks like a child caught with her hand in daddy's wallet. "Ronny, I'm sorry," says Baby, turning to gaze up into the Guildemeister's eyes. "I'm so sorry. I just had to get away. I was scared. I never wanted to hurt you. Don't let him take me back."

Johnny Puke backhands her, knocking her off the bed and slamming her head against the night table. "Shut the fuck up, Baby. Just shut the fuck up. Now, let's see what we got here."

With his lips moving with every number, Johnny Puke fingers the pile of money spread out before him. "I makes it out to be just under thirty-five grand."

"Yeah, I had thirty-eight thousand. She must have spent some of it."

"You had thirty-eight? What about my money? What about my seventy-five thousand?"

"I never took no money from him, Ronny. He's lying," says Baby, crouching in the corner.

"I thought I told you to shut the fuck up, Baby. Look, I'm a reasonable man," says Johnny Puke, turning to Ronny. "What say I give you one thousand dollars and we call it even?"

"But that's what I owe Renée. What about my thirty-eight thousand? This isn't right."

"Hum. You got a point. What you say I give you shit? That sound fair?" asks Johnny Puke, opening his jacket just enough to display the pearl handled forty-four stuck into his waistband.

"Mr. Pucker, this ain't—"

"Get the fuck outta here before I blow your Goddamn head off."

"Don't leave me with him, Ronny. I can't go back. He'll hurt me."

"Shit, I ain't goin' hurt you, Baby, at least not much. You too valuable to me." Then turning again to Ronny, Johnny Puke asks, "You still here?"

Getting a gun in New Orleans is about as difficult as picking up the clap in Vegas, even a high-powered rifle with a scope and silencer. Finding Johnny Puke is even easier. With Ronny's money in his pocket, Johnny Puke is acting the big man, throwing money around the French Quarter like there's no tomorrow. And for Johnny Puke, that's true.

Ronny's surprised at how it comes back so easily: the butt of the rifle pulled snug against his shoulder, the controlled breathing, the gentle squeeze to the trigger, the soft pop of the silenced round speeding from the barrel. Johnny Puke's standing on the balcony of his hotel, watching the sunset over the Mississippi and smoking a celebratory cigar. Then the evening turns redder, and a cigar tumbles nine floors to the parking lot below.

Soon the Guildemeister is seen once again strolling up Royal Street, flashing his golden grillwork at passersby. The gold bowler is perched on top his head, the shiny shoes glide along the narrow sidewalk, and the golden-handled walking stick taps out a syncopated rhythm on the pavement. But now, he has a lady on his arm, a lady dressed in a shimmering gold dress and sporting sparkly shoes with gold stiletto heels. An elegant lady. A lady he calls Baby.

The Story Teller

When I was eight years old, my father told me color had not come into the world until World War II. Before then, the world was black and white and various tints of gray. Supposedly, color, an invention of the Nazis, had been brought to the United States when Jewish scientists like Einstein fled from the Third Reich. That explained why all the photographs before then were in black and white. They were just capturing the world the way it looked in those days. When I asked my father about old paintings that were in color, he explained to me they'd been sprayed later after color had been invented. Before then, they'd been black and white, too.

My father liked to screw with my head. I never really understood why. Maybe it was his twisted sense of humor, maybe it was some kind of power-play, or maybe it was just he had to tell stories.

On my ninth birthday, my father told me he was the second smartest man in the world, edged out only by Elmer Richards, a guy he worked with down at the Jax brewery in the French Quarter. Between the two of them, they knew everything in the world. Everything.

"Go ahead; ask me a question."

"What's the capital of Virginia?" I asked.

"Easy. Richmond."

"Okay. What's the capital of North Dakota?"

"Hmm. That's something Mr. Richards knows."

"What's 230 times 459 times zero?

"Zero," my father answered.

"What's 12 minus six times 43 divided by nine?

"That's another thing that Mr. Richards knows."

This went for several months until I was at the annual company picnic thrown by the beer distributors for Jax employees. I approached Mr. Richards and asked, "What's the capital of North Dakota?"

"What the fuck?"

"Don't swear in front of the kids, Elmer," Mrs. Richards said.

Over the years, I heard all about the albino alligators in the sewers, rats the size of alley cats, and all kinds of body parts found in fast food. Even as an adult, when my father got going on one of his stories, I was never sure what to think.

My father's name was Michael Patrick Doyle, but everyone called him Whitey, due to his pale blond hair that later would turn white with an easy grace. His great-great-great grandfather had fled one of the famines in Ireland and settled in the Irish Channel of New Orleans in the 1840s. They were trades people: blacksmiths, coopers, and day laborers, and in my father's case, a beer bottler. My father was short but with a barrel chest, thick arms, and stout legs. Think of a bantam rooster or James Cagney in 'Yankee Doodle Dandy.' His blue eyes would keep their sparkle almost to the end. My mother Kathleen, my older sister Pat, and my younger brother Tommy were cut from the same cloth. I was the odd man out: dark, tall, and slim. Black Irish, I was told, taking after my mother's father. For a while, growing up, I was convinced that I was the son of an Arab prince or a Latin aristocrat stolen from my bed one night by gypsies and dropped at the door of our double shotgun on lower Fourth Street.

I had left our Irish Channel neighborhood in the late 1960s to go to college up north. The brewery soon shut down, and, after my mother's death, my father shut down, too. He lived on social security and a small pension, and he filled his days by railing at the TV news and then going down to Danny's Bar to reprise his complaints with his cronies. After college, I became a government lawyer in Washington and did okay. Every six months or so, I'd send a check to the old man to supplement his retirement. He never acknowledged the money, and I never expected him to do so, but he did cash the checks.

We'd get together about once a year for the holidays, usually at my older sister Pat's place out in Metairie. She lived in one of those big, brick places out near Lake Pontchartrain. She'd married a rich, oil broker but probably made more money from her Mary Kay franchise than he did from his tankers. At least she did pretty well, judging from the new pink Cadillac parked in her driveway each year. My dad would drive over on Christmas Eve and stay a couple of nights, and my younger brother Tommy and his family would drop by for a meal or two.

I'd take a late flight from DC to New Orleans and then catch a cab for the short ride from the airport over to Pat's house. When I'd walk in the door, my father would look up and wave me over to where he was sitting. "Billy, Billy, you look good. How're you doing? Did you hear that someone over at the Popeye's on St. Charles Avenue found a fried rat in his bucket of chicken?"

"Dad—"

"No really, turns out it was the size of a cat is what I heard."

Or, "Billy, you ain't going to believe this. The whole Kennedy assassination was faked. Turns out JFK had overdosed on all those painkillers he was shooting up for his back. Turned himself into a zombie. Jackie was so pissed about all the bimbos he'd been screwing that she agreed to sit in the open limo next to some dead guy they made up to look like Jack. Then the CIA had their man Oswald pretend to shoot him. Of course, they had rigged the body with some of that Hollywood exploding blood stuff to make it look real. I should've guessed that. No one could've made that shot from the window of the book repository. Anyway, JFK is supposedly still alive at some place outside of Vegas financed by Howard Hughes's guys. You hear that?"

During the winter of 1990, I'd been spending a lot of time over in Chicago on government business. One Friday night in late November, I returned to my Washington apartment just off Dupont Circle to find the answering machine blinking with a message from my sister Pat. "I don't think he's going to make it until Christmas. You better come down if you want to see him again." I packed a carry-on and caught a flight to New Orleans the next day.

When I was growing up, the old neighborhood had been about equally divided between the Irish and the Italians, but over the years, these families moved out to the suburbs near the lake or over to Jefferson Parish in search of safer streets and better schools, and the neighborhood became predominantly poor and black. Crack houses sprang up on every block and the sound of gunfire replaced children's laughter in the streets. Then, in the mid-1970s, there was some interest in reinvesting in the neighborhood by urban pioneers, but with the collapse of the short-lived oil boom in the 1980s, that moment fizzled out.

Through all these years, there were a few Irish holdouts like my father. They refused to leave and could still be found in places like Danny's Bar. A number of the older Italian families had hung on, too. Supposedly, the Deliberti family still ran most of the local rackets as it had when I was growing up. Now, at the beginning of the 1990s, the neighborhood was changing again, being gentrified by young, white, professional couples.

When I called my father to let him know I'd be arriving that afternoon, he asked, "What time?"

"Plane lands at four. I should be at your place by five."

"Meet me at Danny's."

"Danny's? Are you sure you should be going out?"

"What are you, a doctor now? Five to seven, I'm at Danny's. You want to see me, that's where I'll be."

So shortly after five on a windy Saturday in late November, I walked into Danny's looking for my father. Danny's served draft Dixie, boiler makers, and Jameson's, if there was something special to celebrate. You wanted something else, go someplace else, unless of course you were an attractive lady; then Danny might be persuaded to pour a glass of wine. But he wouldn't be happy about it—not that Danny ever seemed to be particularly happy about anything.

As I entered the bar, I was greeted by the familiar smell of stale beer and staler cigarette smoke that always reminded me of feeling up Peggy Harrington. My father had walked in on us sprawled on the living room couch and caught me with my hand up her blouse. I was thirteen. He didn't say anything at the time, but the next day when he got home from work at 4:45, he walked into my room and said, "Come with me."

We walked the five minutes to Danny's in silence. Then, it had been a spring evening, and the air was fragrant with jasmine, which made entering the pungent air of Danny's all the more startling and memorable. We sat in a booth in the rear, and Danny brought my father a shot and a beer. "Bring the boy a beer." Danny didn't say anything, but he did bring the beer.

"Dad, I don't think I'm supposed to be drinking this."

"If you're old enough to get a girl pregnant, you're old enough to drink a beer," he said, throwing back his shot.

"Christ, no one's getting anyone pregnant."

"Don't swear, Goddamn it. It's time I told you the facts of life."

"I know the facts of life. Why don't we just skip the discussion and enjoy the beer."

"Don't mouth off at me. You don't know shit."

"I know shit."

"Didn't I just tell you not to swear?" he said, clenching his fists before him on the table. "Anyways, I don't want you feeling up the Harrington girl no more. She's a nice kid, and I don't want to see her getting pregnant or nothing."

"I don't think you can get a girl pregnant from copping a feel."

"What'd I say about mouthing off? Anyways, it just shows you don't know nothing. Turns out sperm's got a long life. You can jerk off one day, and don't even try to tell me you don't do it, and the next day you can still have live sperm on your hand, maybe under your nails or somewhere. You cop a feel and get some on her and then she takes a shower and it washes down and gets inside her and before you know it, she's pregnant. I heard it from a doctor," he said, tapping his finger on the table.

"But that doesn't make any sense. Wouldn't the same thing happen if you just held her hand? Why isn't everyone pregnant?"

"It's got something to do with body heat. Turns out sperm needs to stay in a warm place like between a woman's breasts. Something like that."

"But what about before then, when it's—"

"Look, don't argue. You think you're smarter than a doctor or something?"

"No, it's just—"

34

"It's just nothing. End of subject." He drained his beer, and setting the glass down, he turned toward the bar and said, "Danny, another round here."

As I wondered whatever had become of Peggy Harrington after all these years, my eyes adjusted to the barroom's gloom, and I spied my father sitting at the end of the bar. As I approached, he turned toward the door and spotted me. He looked a lot older than I remembered from last Christmas. He got off the stool and stood tilting to one side as if his left hip had lost some of its will to support him. He held out his hand and shook mine, nodding toward a vacant booth. "Two Jamesons, Danny," he said over his shoulder as we made our way to the rear booth.

When Danny brought over the drinks and set them before us, he said, "Good to see you, Billy."

"Same here, Danny."

"When you see these empty," my father said, "bring us a couple more."

Danny nodded and returned to his station behind the bar, idly wiping a soiled rag across the bar top for the millionth time.

"Did you hear about that Chink place down the street?"

"Chinese. No."

"Turns out they been stir-frying cats and passing it off as beef. Damndest thing."

"Dad, I don't think—"

"Doesn't matter," he said waving off the comment and lifting his glass. "To your mother, may she rest in peace."

We drank in silence for a moment before he spoke again. "You talk to Pat?"

"Yeah."

"She tell you I'm dying?"

"Yeah."

"Turns out it's true."

"You never know—"

"I know, Billy. I know."

There was nothing to say for a moment; then he said, "Look. There's something I got to tell you. I should've told you a long time ago, but, well…. Anyway, before you were born, but after Pat was born, I was working at the brewery and involved in the union. Turns out the Deliberti Family had a lock on the organization, so if you wanted to get along, you went along, if you know what I mean. I never did nothing illegal or anything, but I did look the other way once or twice. Anyway, we sort of got to know the Delibertis pretty good at that time. Around then, I did something pretty dumb. I had a little fling with the nurse at the brewery. It was stupid and didn't really mean nothing, but it happened and your mother found out. She took Pat and went to stay with her mother. I thought she was going to leave me."

"Dad, you don't need to—"

"Yeah, I do." But he quieted long enough for Danny to set down two fresh drinks and to pick up our empties. Then he continued. "One day on the job, I get a message the foreman wants to see me. I go down to his office, but when I get there he ain't there. Instead, sitting in his chair is Frankie Deliberti, the brother to Carmine, the head of the union. Frankie is the head of the Family, if you get my meaning. He's about my age at the time, thirty-five or so. In fact, me and him went to school together, and as I said, we'd become sort of close to the Delibertis, though honestly, I was closer to Carmine. Anyway, he motions me to a chair and says, 'How you been, Whitey?'"

"Good. Okay. How you doing, Mr. Deliberti?"

"Please. It's me, Frankie. We've known each other too long."

"Sure, Frankie. Anything you say."

"This trouble between you and your missus, Kathleen. It's not good. You have a baby, Patricia. She needs a father."

"I agree, Frankie, but it's not my call. I made a mistake. Kathleen can't seem to see it in her heart to forgive me."

"Could you forgive her for such a thing?"

"Jesus. It's different for a guy, you know."

"Sometimes it is, and sometimes it isn't. Your heart big enough for such forgiveness? It's an important question, Whitey."

"Yeah. I think my heart would be big enough for such forgiveness."

"Kathleen talked with my wife. She wants to come back to you but only if you could forgive her like she is willing to forgive you."

"She wants to come back?"

"Yeah, but your heart has got to be big enough. You've got to understand her forgiveness. To appreciate it. Your heart big enough?"

"It's big enough."

"Sure?"

"Sure."

"Okay. I'll make a call. She should be waiting for you when you get home from your shift."

"Jesus, thanks Frankie. And thanks to Mrs. Deliberti, I mean Maria."

"Okay. Big heart?"

"Big heart. Yeah."

My father took another belt from his Jameson's and nodded toward Danny. After our glasses were full again, he said, "So what do you think? Weird, huh?"

"I guess. I never knew you and Ma had separated."

"Yeah, three months. And it gets weirder. After she returns, it turns out she's pregnant."

"Turns out she's pregnant? Christ, Dad, what are you saying?"

My father nodded looking down at his glass. He took a sip from his drink and looking up said, "Yeah, Billy, turns out you're not mine. I mean, I'm your father, but I'm not."

"Dad, if this is another of your crazy stories—"

"You think I'd joke about something like this."

"No. I don't know. Maybe. Jesus. So, who's my father?"

"I don't know. Your ma never told me, but if I had to guess, I'd guess you're the Italian's kid.

"The Italian's kid?"

"Yeah, Frankie Deliberti's."

I leaned back in the booth and looked around Danny's. Everything was familiar yet startlingly altered, kind of like the shock I got every time I returned to the home of my youth and saw it was so much smaller and dingier than my childhood memory. Across the table, my father stared into his whiskey, his shoulders stooped as if a burden he had hoped to lift had instead become heavier.

I returned to Washington the next day, my head spinning. I decided my father and I would have another sit down over the holidays and that I would get to the bottom of all this, but as my sister Pat had predicted, I never got the chance.

My father died a week later.

We held a small service on a cloudy day in early December. A few of Pat's and my brother Tommy's friends showed up along with a large contingent from Danny's, who, with their bleary eyes, looked like they had started the wake early. It wasn't until

Christmas when I returned again to New Orleans that I had a chance to sit down with Pat to discuss my own situation.

She was sipping a cup of tea at the kitchen table, recovering from all the Christmas day craziness. "Want a cup?" she asked, pushing a stray strand of hair off of her face.

"No thanks. I'm fine. Nice day."

"It was a nice day, wasn't it? Though it was strange not having Dad here. The house seemed quieter. No surprise there."

We sat in silence for a few minutes, and then I asked, "Did Dad ever mention anything to you about him splitting with Ma for a while back when you were little and before I was born?"

"What? No. Where'd you hear something like that?" she asked looking over the rim of her cup.

"Or what about me not really being his kid?"

"Whoa. What's this all about, Billy?"

So, I told her of my last drink with my father and the revelations he had put on the table.

"And you believed him?"

"Why would he make up something like that?"

"Come on, Billy. Are we talking about the same guy? Why would he make up stories about JFK's assassination, or loups-garous sneaking into town on a Mardi Gras float looking for little children to eat, or the moon walk being faked in Las Vegas? He even told me once that I was adopted."

"Really?"

"Turns out, I'd been left on their doorstop by the fairies."

"Oh. Well, that's a bit different."

"Jesus, Billy. Why are you taking this stuff seriously? The old man was a kook. Loveable, but a kook nonetheless. We all grew up with his crazy stories. I admit this one is at the top of kookiness, but it's just another of his fantasies. Why are you letting it bother you?" she asked, as she stood and placed her cup in the sink.

"Well, for one thing, look at you and Tommy. You're both fair. Reddish hair, freckles, short. Look at me. Dark hair, dark skin, and tall. I don't look like the rest of you."

"Black Irish," she said, leaning back against the sink with her hands behind her.

"I know. I've heard it all my life. Ma's father was as dark as the Irish could be. Descended from the Moorish invaders or something. Black Irish. Yeah, I know. Don't you think that was a little too convenient?

"Come on, Billy."

"And how about when we were growing up. Irish and Italian kids only mixed at school. Afterward, if an Irish kid ran into a bunch of Italians, he'd get the shit beat out him."

"Same for an Italian kid."

"Sure. That's my point. But I never got beaten up. I even got cornered a couple of times over on Annunciation, but Tony Deliberti always intervened and said, 'Not him.' It was as if the word was out that I was to be spared."

"Yeah, but Tony was in your class. You told me you took the rap for him when he shot the rubber band at the nun and she thought it was you. You never ratted him out and got a whipping and a week's detention, as I remember."

"That's not enough to prevent a beating."

"You don't think?"

"I never really thought about it before, but there must have been something else going on."

She sat down again at the table and took my hands in hers. "Look, Billy, drop it. It was nothing. Ma would never have done anything like that. It wasn't only the times; it was her. She just wouldn't have. You're upset over nothing. It was just the old man and one of his crazy stories."

But I couldn't drop it, so two days later on a rainy morning, I went to see Frankie Deliberti. It took some doing. Frankie Deliberti isn't the kind of guy you just drop in on. I'd finally called his son and my old classmate, Tony, and he'd called back saying his father would see me. I'm not sure what I expected, maybe a dark café and some old gray men leaning over their espressos, or an untidy office in a warehouse with an electric space heater buzzing in the corner. I certainly didn't expect the modern office building with the metal detector, the pretty receptionist, the sign-in form, and the laminated visitor's badge.

When the elevator stopped on the tenth floor, I stepped out into a reception area with floor-to-ceiling glass and a deep plush burgundy carpet. Another pretty receptionist sat behind a walnut desk, but before I could approach her, Tony rose from a silk upholstered chair and came toward me.

"Billy, good to see you."

"Likewise."

We shook hands, and he smiled with what seemed genuine warmth. "Sorry to hear about your father. My condolences."

"Thanks. I appreciate you setting up this meeting."

"For someone from the neighborhood, it's no problem. But let me show you in. The old man's running a bit behind schedule, as usual."

Tony opened the door, and I entered. I heard the door shut behind me. I glanced over my shoulder and saw that Tony was gone. Frankie Deliberti sat behind his chrome and glass desk. He was much as I remembered. Tall and elegant, as I stepped closer I could see deep lines around his eyes, and his once black hair, still combed straight back, was now streaked with gray. His blue, pinstriped suit was impeccably tailored, but his red tie looked faded and was loosened at the collar. On his left, floor-to-ceiling glass overlooked the French Quarter; on his right, the dark wood-paneled wall held a collection of civic plaques and photos of him with local and national politicians. He rose with a smile and came from behind the desk and shook my hand and placed his left hand on my shoulder. "Billy, it's good to see you. I was sorry to hear about the death of your father. He was a good man."

I thanked him as he ushered me into a comfortable, beige leather chair and sat down in a similar one across from me. We discussed the weather, my job in Washington, and a few other pleasantries, and he selected an apple from a bowl of fruit on the table between us. Taking a folding knife out of his pocket, he cut a slice of apple and pierced it with the tip of the blade of the knife and pointed it in my direction.

"No, thanks," I said.

He put the slice of apple into his mouth and chewing said, "So, Billy, what can I do for you?"

He listened patiently while I told him my story, interrupting me only twice to get a clarification about a date and a place. Then, he sat back and studied the ceiling for a while. Looking down, he noticed that some of the juice from the apple had dripped on to the sleeve of his jacket. Wiping at it with his hand, he got up and walked to the window and looked out over the Quarter. He was still staring out the window when he asked, "So, what do you want from me, Billy?"

"The truth."

"Ah, the truth," he said, turning to look at me. "Truth is your old man and me were never all that close. Sure, at one point we had some business together, union stuff. He and your mother came over to the house a couple of times. Picnics, cookouts, crawfish boils, that sort of thing. Your mother and my wife, God rest their souls, got along pretty good. Not close, really, but they had stuff in common. Both had small girls and were starting their families. Both had difficult husbands but difficult in different ways.

"I remember they had some problems, like you said. Some kind of a fight. I never really knew what it was about, but there was talk. Irish. Italians. We've had our differences, but we were all Catholics. Divorce was never an option, and separations weren't much of an alternative either in those days. So, they got back together. That's what I know."

"With all due respect, Mr. Deliberti," I said, standing and joining him by the windows, "that doesn't really answer my question. According to my father, my mother returned to the marriage pregnant. With me."

"Yeah. You said that," he said, patting my arm and walking over to his desk. Sitting on a corner, he continued, "Your father was quite the story teller. He once told me the Irish invented spaghetti. We had quite an argument about it. I, of course, insisted it was the Italians. Only years later did I learn that it was probably the Chinese, but that's neither here nor there. My point is your father could spin quite a yarn."

"But the truth. Is his story real or not? Are you my father?"

"So, there it is," he said, standing and spreading his arms wide. "You Irish are always so direct. We Italians like to dance around a subject a bit before getting to it, but that's neither here nor there. Anyhow. So, what if I say, 'No, I'm not your father?' You going to believe that, or will you still have your doubts? What if I say, 'Yes?' You might believe me today, but later you'll think about your mother and doubt that she would have had an affair with anyone, especially an Italian. It just wasn't done in those days… so you wonder. Maybe that old Deliberti was just fucking with your mind. Maybe he had an old grudge against your father, something you never knew about, and this was his chance to get even. Maybe the woman your father had his affair with wasn't just some nurse at the brewery but someone close to old Deliberti. Very close. Maybe I got a big grudge."

"I just want the truth."

"The truth. You want the truth. Well, here's another story. Sit down."

We sat in the leather chairs again, and he leaned toward me. "After your mother left your father, your father descended into the bottle the way you Irish can do. Don't look at me that way. Some of these things they say about people are true. You Irish have a fondness for drink, violence, song, story-telling, and hard work. We Italians like eating, violence, song, story-telling, and not so hard work. Sure, sure, I know, we're not supposed to say these things today, but that don't make them less true.

"Anyway, your father drinks more than usual, and his usual was a lot in any case. He's sad; he drinks more. He's angry; he drinks more. He's lonely; he drinks more. He begins to miss days at work. He suffers black outs.

"One night he goes to your mother in such a state. She feels sorrow; she feels pity. She takes him to bed, but she doesn't yet feel forgiveness, so he goes home alone. The next morning, he remembers being with your mother, but he thinks it was only a dream. Later, she returns to him. There's a baby. It's you."

He leaned back in his chair, clasping his hands and laying them across his chest. "There. That's another story. But these are all just stories. Why are you so worried about all the stories others tell you, even those told by your father? Make up your own story. Live your own story. Now, you will have to excuse me," he said standing. "I'm late for a meeting across town."

The plane back to Washington was full. I sat at the window, and a small boy, maybe six or seven, with light blond hair falling into his eyes, squirmed into the middle seat beside me. His mother wrestled an oversized bag into the overhead compartment and fell into the aisle seat with a sigh. After take-off, I leaned against the window and stared out at the night lights far below. The muffled roar of the engines and the slight vibration of the plane hurling through the black sky rocked me kindly. The flight attendant brought a coloring book and a pack of five crayons, and the boy tore open the box and went to work. His mother snored lightly beside him. I looked over and saw that he had drawn a picture of a man and a woman holding the hands of a small child between them.

"Nice picture," I said.

"Thanks. That's me and my mom and my dad. We're going home. My dad's going to meet us at the airport."

"You draw very well."

"Yeah, I like pictures. Red's my favorite color," he said, holding up the red crayon for me to see.

"Yeah, red's a good one. Did you know that color was only invented a few years ago? Probably just before you were born."

"Really?"

"Yeah, before then everything was in black and white. Turns out color was an unexpected by-product of the invention of the computer. If you like, I'll tell you the story."

The One-Upper

Dog soup usually does it. But if it doesn't, I have one more culinary oddity in my historical pantry that I can place on the table.

We're dining with Trish and Robert (never Bob) in their newly renovated double shotgun house in the Uptown neighborhood of New Orleans. Trish is an old, college friend of my wife from Massachusetts. Robert is Trish's new husband, whom we've only met a couple of times. He's amiable enough, with a big laugh and a belly to match though he has one annoying trait. He's a One-Upper. At an earlier get-together, when I'd mentioned I once ate two hundred oysters over the course of a long afternoon at a Cajun wedding south of Lafayette, Robert said, "Ha! I once ate a Webster's Dictionary to try to get into the Guinness Book of Records." When I told the story of a thirty-hour college road trip from Baltimore to Corpus Christi crammed into a '63 VW Bug with two buddies, Robert said, "Ha! I once drove an old Caddy hearse from New York to Los Angeles in three days with only a bottle of Dexedrine for company." When I mentioned seeing the sunrise over the Haleakala Crater on Maui, Robert said, "Ha! I once saw the sunset from the top of Mount Everest." Okay, maybe he didn't really say that, but you can bet he said something else just as outrageous.

Tonight, sitting around their candle-lit, maple dining room table, in addition to the four of us, are the Jamesons, Diane and Claude. Diane's quite the dish, with meticulous make-up and every one of her shining blond hairs neatly in place. She's a bit overdressed for this informal evening in a shiny, green silk dress, exposing a generous amount of cleavage. This has not gone unnoticed by Robert, who in a couple of unguarded moments looks as if he'd like to dive right in and take up permanent residence. Her husband, Claude, is more retiring with a pasty complexion and a comb-over that looks as if it was styled by a Dairy Queen soft-serve dispenser. The Jamesons live down the street from Trish and Robert, and this is the first time we've met them. They're CPAs, running their accounting firm out of a small office on Magazine Street.

The dinner's been pleasant enough, blackened snapper, mashed potatoes, and baby carrots, with a nice Fumé Blanc. We're just finishing our apple tart, and we've gone through the usual banter covering, "How did you two meet?" and "Children?" and "What are you reading?" and "What's your favorite movie?" We already know about our careers, where we live, and how we got here, and it's still too early in the new friendships to wade into political and religious waters. We're still exploring safe ground, still sounding each other out.

Looking for an interesting and non-controversial topic to enjoy with our coffee, someone raises the question, "What's the strangest meal you've ever eaten?" Maybe it was me, coming to any discussion of exotic meals holding good cards. My parents were immigrants to New York from Scotland in the closing days of World War II, not the ditch-digging, lift-yourself-up-by-your-bootstrap variety of transplants, but more the educated, sophisticated sort, if the idea of a sophisticated Scot isn't too much of an oxymoron to swallow. I point this out because their background meant they enjoyed many traditional Scottish foods but were also open to new and occasionally bizarre culinary adventures.

I grew up in the 1950s thinking it normal to breakfast on porridge, lunch on barley soup and a meat pie, and dine on boiled potatoes and any one of an assortment of organ meats, such as liver, kidneys, tripe, or tongue. For special occasions, we might have scrambled eggs with calf's brains, blood sausage, or a nice kipper for breakfast, breaded herring for lunch, and even the Haggis for dinner, when one could be found. Of course, we didn't always eat like this. Other more normal Scottish-acceptable fare was offered, such as roast beef, leg of lamb, or pork chops. But still, more often than not, some offal stuffed in a casing or salted fish or cured meat would be on the table.

Beyond this traditional Scottish fare, my parents enjoyed escargot and frog legs from France, mulligatawny soup from India, calamari from Italy, and moo goo gai pan from China, at a time when chop suey was still all the rage. For my afternoon snack, my mother might open a can of smoked mussels or a tin of Portuguese sardines packed in mustard sauce. My folks were drinking Pouilly-Fuisse and serving stinky Gorgonzola while most of the neighbors were making do with Rheingold and Velveeta. When we'd head to Long Island for two weeks in the summer, I'd stand alongside my father devouring raw clams and oysters and steamed crabs and lobsters while my friends back home were scarfing down bologna sandwiches or boiled hot dogs.

As for the bizarre, my mother fell in love with fresh fruits upon her arrival in the New World, especially bananas which I came to understand were a bit of a rarity in Glasgow during the war. I thought nothing of eating a breakfast of mashed bananas in orange juice, called simply banana-orange, into which we'd dip hot buttered toast. Sliced bananas with mayonnaise on white bread became a luncheon staple. Even her holiday trifle dessert was modified to include a layer of ripe banana between the

Byrd's custard, the Scotch-soaked pound cake, and the black currant jam.

All this set the stage for a life of adventurous eating. I didn't rebel by insisting on hamburgers and apple pie. No, I wanted to raise the ante, and I got the chance through travel, sampling many exotic foods along the way. So when the dinner conversation turns to the strangest thing you ever ate, I'm well positioned to clean the table.

I open our after-dinner conversation with, "Termites, alive, right off the nest in a jungle in Belize,"

"Ha!" Robert, the One-Upper, jumps right in and says, "I once ate a fried tarantula in Bangkok."

"Ever try the jelly fish in Hong Kong?" I ask, leaning forward.

"Delicious. Ever eaten sheep's head?" he responds, resting his forearms on the table.

"In Morocco once. The eyeball is especially tasty," I lie, for in fact, it's like trying to swallow a lump of gelatinous snot, definitely an acquired taste.

In fact, people will ingest the damnedest things. In Taiwan, you can buy bottles of snake wine—wine with a venomous snake pickled inside the bottle. In Indonesia, if you can afford it, you might get the chance to sip Kopi Luwak—a drink brewed from coffee beans that have been digested and defecated by the Luwak civet, a catlike creature. In Ecuador, you might dine on roast Guinea Pig. In Sardinia, it might be Casu Marzu, a sheep milk cheese crawling with live maggots. In the Philippines, the Balut, a chicken or duck fetus about to emerge from its shell is considered quite the treat. Durian is a popular fruit in Southeast Asia. Some say it tastes like strawberry, almonds, or vanilla custard. Others compare it more to rancid garlic or burnt plastic. However, everyone seems to agree its odor is a cross between old, wet, dirty socks and pig manure. The smell is so offensive that it is banned from most public places. Now, I've not eaten any of these, though I would. Well, maybe not the Casu Marzu or the Balut, but I have eaten my assortment of oddities: Baby eels in Norway, birds nest soup (which after all gets its texture from the saliva of the Swift), crawfish here in New Orleans (which are really just aquatic cockroaches if you think about it), peacock in India (yes, it tasted like chicken—a very tough, old, dry one), and camel stew in Marrakech. I once had sushi in Tokyo. Not remarkable in itself, except that the sushi was being served from a living carp that crossed its eyes with every slice.

"Rattlesnake," says Robert.

"Sea Cucumber," I respond, knowing Robert will recognize this for what it is—a sea slug.

"Sea urchin."

"Grilled sparrows."

Everyone else at the table has grown quiet. Diane, her complexion now rivaling the green of her dress, holds her napkin to her mouth, its length obscuring her cleavage, much to Robert's evident annoyance. Apparently, this type of high-stakes food one-upsmanship doesn't appeal to the ladies. And poor Claude, sitting back and busying himself by patting his comb-over on his pasty, bald pate, has seemingly decided to bow out after a timid offering of chocolate covered ants.

It's now time to go all in and one-up the One-Upper. One of the most remarkable meals I ever enjoyed, and enjoy it I did, was a duck dinner in Beijing. If you've ordered Peking duck in a Chinese restaurant, most likely you've been served crispy duck breast you roll up in a pale rice pancake with some dark Hoisin sauce and a few green scallions. And, indeed, that was one of the courses I had in Beijing, but that course was preceded with duck feet, sort of like chewing on rubber bands, and duck tongues, far more tender. Slowly but surely, we made our way through every part of the duck to end up with the pièce de résistance; duck brains on the half-shell, or in this case, the half-skull.

I mention the duck brains, figuring that will shut down Robert.

"Kittens," Robert answers.

"Kittens? You ate kittens?"

"Well, not really me. It was my great uncle, a World War II veteran. He told me he was once so hungry that, when he and his platoon came upon a barn with a new litter of kittens, they made a stew."

Well, this clearly doesn't count. We haven't spelled out the rules, but the subject obviously isn't the weirdest thing anyone, anywhere has eaten. If that were the case, I'd have ended the contest long ago with the psycho from New York who killed his wife, made chili, and fed her remains to the homeless in Thompkins Square in the East Village, bragging all the time, "The secret's in the sauce." No, we're plainly talking about our personal experiences. But smelling desperation, I decide to be magnanimous and to ignore Robert's clear infraction.

"Dog soup," I say. "I went to dinner with some folks in Seoul and wondered why everyone was snickering when I ordered a second helping of the soup. Then they told me, 'Puppy Soup.'"

I look over at my wife, Ann. Apparently, she's seen me play this game once too often, for she's rolling her eyes at our distressed hostess, Trish, who realizes her carefully prepared dinner has been long forgotten. I know I'll be hearing about this later, about how I shouldn't have risen to Robert's challenges, about how I shouldn't let my competitive nature get the best of me. But what's a guy to do? All the more reason to settle back into my chair, relieved that I won't have to play my final card, for I do have one more culinary oddity, but I'm loath to employ it unless absolutely necessary.

"Ha. Rooster testicles," Robert says, folding his hands over his belly, evidently not yet ready to throw in the towel.

"Uh?"

"Yep, rooster testicles," he says, thoroughly enjoying the slack-jawed expressions on the ladies' faces and my own squirming discomfort. "Had 'em in Snake Alley in Taiwan. Ever been there?"

As a matter of fact, I have. Snake Alley is an infamous market in Taipei, where eager hosts take their foreign visitors to gross them out. There, the wealthy can buy snake blood extracted right in front of you, turtles, lizards, and various rare herbs and medicinals, all promising to make the lady's complexion glow and the man's erection rise. "Make your wife very happy," guarantees each vendor. Unfortunately, other things are for sale, too, whether real or fake: black bear pancreas, powdered rhinoceros horn, ivory potions, and a host of other bits and parts of every endangered species on the planet.

Obviously, I missed the stall for the rooster balls. Since it's obvious Robert is unwilling to concede with dignity, I reluctantly say, "I once ate a tiger's heart."

I say this with what I hope is just the right tone of shame and humility while at the same time sneaking a peak at the crestfallen Robert.

The story is true. It's a long story, and one for another day, but the result was that in 1960, when I was fifteen, I accompanied an Austrian big game hunter into the remote regions of northern India to track a Bengal tiger that had been terrorizing a local village. Tigers were still roaming the wilds in India during that time though people were beginning to become concerned with their declining numbers. A decade later, the Indian government would ban tiger hunting except in the rare cases where tigers killed people and their capture was infeasible. Long story short, the tiger was killed. Much to my surprise, the cook served an evening stew of meat and vegetables. The Austrian hunter shared his celebratory meal with me, and I had a mouthful or two of tiger heart.

I smile smugly, savoring the look of shock and awe on the other diners' faces.

"Not so fast." Our somnolent CPA, Claude, leaving his comb-over to care for itself, sits up and speaks.

"Hmm?" I murmur, my palms turning damp.

"I once had bull penis soup in Shanghai," he says.

I feel sucker punched, this devastating blow appearing from nowhere. Our fellow diners all gag appreciatively. They look away from me and turn their attention to the penis eater, now sitting erect and gloating at the other end of the table. By their postures, I can tell that my confession of dining on an endangered species has lost their support and that their initial shock and awe has turned to derision. They have a new champion. Even Robert, so glum a moment ago, has perked up, smirking. As I watch my triumph evaporate, I happen to glance at Diane in her shiny green silk dress, her cleavage once more exposed. She has brightened, and her complexion now seems to glow. She gazes at her victorious husband, a hint of a smile playing across her lips. Perhaps she's remembering an after-dinner night in Shanghai when her well-fed husband made her very happy.

The Guy in the Box

I wanted to scream. They were all in denial: my wife, Kathy, her mother, we called her Mother Rita, and her father, Louie. I drove through the snowy night, gripping the steering wheel tighter trying to keep the car steady on the slippery Rhode Island highway. At the same time, I struggled to keep my impatience in check as the rest of the family chatted away amiably as if nothing was off center. Laughing and jabbering, all in denial. Well, maybe not Louie with his hold on reality slipping away so rapidly. Denial may have been beyond his capabilities. I felt like the proverbial one-eyed man in the land of the blind, trying, as I had been for months, to lead the family to accept Louie's dementia, but no one was seeing it my way.

"Oh, that's just Louie," Mother Rita would say. She was a fireplug of women with iron-clad opinions and a perpetual smile welded to her face. "He's always been a scatter-brain. You should have known him when we first married. Honestly, I don't know how that man dressed himself until I came along."

Kathy, as much as I love her, was almost as bad. Slim and graceful with legs from here to tomorrow, she'd inherited her father's height. She'd also inherited his inquisitiveness, gentleness, and befuddled impulsiveness. I usually found her Type B personality an attractive counterweight to my own Type A well-organized one. Okay, so sometimes my orderliness crossed the line into compulsiveness, and sometimes Kathy's spontaneity looked more like chaos. Usually we struck a nice complementary balance, but this evening, her easygoing approach irked me as the decline of her father went ignored.

"Dad's just a little eccentric. His head's always been in the clouds. He'd be tinkering with one of his inventions in the garage workroom, like his system to generate power from tap water and Tabasco sauce when all the lights would go out because he forgot to pay the electricity bill. Now with his hearing going, it seems he's more disoriented. That's just Dad."

Okay, they had a point. He was a bit of a kook, always had been—sort of the absent-minded professor/mad scientist type. And he'd had his successes in his unconventional way. He'd registered something like two hundred patents and made a pretty good living off the royalty checks from his inventions. They ranged from a cooling system for silicon superconductors to the more prosaic Mice-a-Matic, a device for cutting vegetables in the shape of Disney cartoon characters. You'd be amazed at the market for something like that.

But there was eccentric, and then there was weird. A psychiatrist once told me that misplacing your car keys is forgetfulness; forgetting what car keys are for is dementia. I wasn't sure Louie even knew what a car was for anymore as he sat in the back seat humming to himself, but no one listened to me.

Ahead, through near blinding snow, I spied the lighted sign announcing Campbell's funeral parlor. I eased into the drive and pulled up next to the snow-packed awning leading to the front door. Ted and Gracie had been Louie and Rita's neighbors for over thirty years. Ted had dropped dead at the senior center during an afternoon screening of Hitchcock's "The Trouble with Harry." Campbell's was the oldest funeral home in Providence, the one where everyone who was anyone went to be laid out. Of course, neither Ted nor Gracie were really on the social register, but Ted had made it clear over the years it was to be Campbell's for him when the day came. So, Campbell's it was.

Ted had been well liked in the area. He was always willing to run an errand, pickup someone's mail, or loan out a garden tool, Good Neighbor Ted, a well-deserved endearment.

After his death, Mother Rita rallied Kathy and some of the neighbors to coordinate the delivery of an endless supply of casseroles to Gracie every evening promptly at six. Nobody but me seemed concerned that Louie suggested more than once that they have Good Neighbor Ted and Gracie over for drinks.

"Oh, you know Dad, he's forgetful. He's just reminiscing about the good old days when the four of them hung out together." Kathy would not be moved, to say nothing of Mother Rita, who seemed to be entering a parallel universe all her own.

As the snow fell harder, I watched Kathy, Mother Rita, and Louie make their way to the entrance, holding on to each other for support and doing a herky-jerky waltz as they navigated the icy walkway. Once they were safely inside, I pulled into the half-full parking lot and managed to slide into a space not too far from the front door. I'd neglected to put on my boots, and the snow was high enough to cover my shoes and soak my socks before I made my way inside.

A blast of hot air hit me. Wouldn't a funeral home keep the thermostat low in deference to the recently departed? Refrigeration seemed a wise course of action, but I guess the directors were more interested in the comfort of the paying customers—the loved ones.

The foyer was dimly lit as befitted the occasion. Flowers graced the polished tables, and the dark wood of the walls gleamed in the quiet light. A pale man in a black suit greeted me, pumping my hand up and down while tisk-tisking his head side-to-side. His smile was at half-mast, apparently ready to broaden if I thought the occasion a blessing... or to escape into a frown if I was feeling a loss. I just nodded, leaving him in that anteroom of emotion as he pointed me to the left and the viewing room.

The widow, Gracie, stood in the doorway dressed in black, her hair lightly blued. Two smudges of rouge sat high on her cheeks, and she clutched a lace hanky wadded in her left hand. An elderly couple, whom I recognized from one or another backyard gathering but whose names eluded me, were consoling her. I joined them.

"Too soon, too soon," said the elderly gentleman. His words had that panicked timber that comes from seeing the Conductor on the Last Train to Eternity jostling down the aisle toward your seat yelling, "Tickets, tickets."

"Such a loss, such a loss," said the elderly woman, patting Gracie's arm.

"He'll be dearly missed," I said, adding my own cliché. "Please don't hesitate to call us."

Gracie nodded and smiled weakly, dabbing the soiled hanky at her nose. As other mourners joined us, I gave Gracie's arm one more pat and made my way into the viewing room.

Illuminated by several recessed spotlights, a beautiful, walnut casket trimmed in brass stood at the front of the room. The lid was raised and Good Neighbor Ted lay nestled in fine white silk. He looked good. In fact, he looked better than he had in years. His hair was neatly combed, his suit pressed, his cheeks rosy, and his hands, folded across his chest, beautifully manicured. I paused for a moment before the casket then made my way to my seat next to Kathy.

Kathy took my hand as I looked around the room. I wasn't quite sure what to expect. I knew the actual church service and burial were scheduled for the following day, so I supposed we'd just sit there for a few minutes bowing our heads respectfully before driving over to Tony's, our favorite Italian restaurant, for a nice plate of lasagna and a glass of Chianti. I bowed my head.

Probably as a result of the heat in the room, my eyes were soon shut, and my head bowed more than was required for the solemn occasion. I may have dozed off; I'm not really sure, but my head snapped back, and my eyes popped open when Louie spoke.

"Who's the guy in the box?" Louie asked one and all, not employing his inside voice as circumstances warranted, but in his I'm-hard-of-hearing-so-I-talk-real-loud voice.

There was a collective gasp from the mourners, and I thought, well that nails it; surely the demented cat is out of the bag now.

But I had underestimated Mother Rita, who calmly said, "Oh, Louie, that's Good Neighbor Ted. You remember."

Well, maybe that didn't nail it after all. Mother Rita still didn't get it. Maybe I'd missed something. Maybe she was as nutty as he. I caught Kathy's eye and gave her my best 'Are you hearing what I'm hearing?' look. She smiled back at me and leaned over, patting my knee. "It's okay. It's just Dad," she whispered. Just Dad! What was she thinking?

"Ted? Ted!" Louie yelled. "What the fuck you doing sleeping in that box? Get out of there."

And with that, Louie sprang for the casket with Mother Rita at his heels, Kathy at her heels, and me bringing up the rear. The widow rose from her chair in the front row, a look of horror slapped across her face. Her expression almost saved the day. Louie stopped in his tracks when he came abreast of her.

"Gracie. How are you doing? Long time no see. What have you guys been up to? Jesus, we've got to have you and Ted over for dinner."

Gracie nodded numbly. Louie pivoted on his heel and stepped up to the coffin.

"Ted, wake up. Show me how this thing works."

Then he was on all fours crawling under the casket, Mother Rita right behind him, trying to grab hold of his ankle. As she scooted after him, her black dress rode up around her hips, presenting her ample hindquarters to the assembled mourners. I averted my gaze. Scurrying around to the other side of the coffin, I intercepted Louie.

There was a crash, and I looked over just in time to see the widow clutch at her chest and faint backwards, taking down a row of chairs and most of her immediate family. The distraction gave us time to smile and nod at everyone and make our escape into the night.

The sky had cleared, and the streets were quiet, the sounds of the night muffled by the newly fallen snow. We drove in silence for a while, the only noise being the swish of the tires on the carpeted roadway. Then Louie spoke from the backseat.

"Sorry, I got a little bit worked up back there."

"That's okay, Louie," Mother Rita said. "It was an emotional occasion."

"Yeah. I gotta tell you… when I saw Ted sleeping on the couch while the rest of us were wiggling around on those hard-backed chairs, I got excited. Yep, that's a very nice couch."

"That's fine, Dad," Kathy said. "Why don't you rest a while? It's been a long day."

"Yeah, but that couch. I can make a better one… maybe use plastics. Make one of the sides hinged, so you can get in and out easily—and the lid. What's with that?"

"Mr. Inventor," Mother Rita said. "Always thinking." And with that, Louie rested his head on Mother Rita's shoulder and closed his eyes. Soon Mother Rita was sleeping, too.

"Kathy—"

She reached over and squeezed my leg. "Not yet."

"Not yet?"

"Look at them together back there," she said. "You know we're all a little bit crazy at times—"

"I think that scene at the funeral parlor was more than being a little—"

"You know there's more than one way to see that. There's Mom's way—refusing to see anything out of the ordinary. There's another way that would destroy this family, as we know it. Or we can see it as Dad being just Dad—but more so—and deal with the 'more so' until a time when we no longer can. Then, maybe soon, we'll have to pick another story, but for tonight, can't we say that's 'Just Dad?' What's the harm in sticking to that story for one more night?"

I looked in the mirror. Mother Rita cradled Louie's head in her arms. Louie snored lightly. Mother Rita's eyes were closed, a trace of a smile resting on her lips.

"Just Dad," I said.

"Just Dad," Kathy answered, her hand brushing the back of my head.

Salt

O n the last day of school before summer vacation, Mrs. Cronin allowed her second-grade students to bring their pets to class. There were hissing cats and slobbering dogs, parakeets and goldfish, a reluctant hamster, and two rabbits, one black and one white. In amongst all the hustle and bustle stood Theodore balancing his ant farm. The other kids bent down to examine the Plexiglas container and frowned.

"What kind of a pet is ants?" asked Nelson Taylor.

"My kind," said Theodore. And it was true. Theodore liked things small, which was good, for due to some 'problems at birth,' Theodore would always be the smallest child in his class. Rather than hiding from his smallness, Theodore seemed to celebrate it, and his parents, both normal-sized, accepted his small ways with good humor and encouraged his downsized interests.

In third grade, while they were learning about circuses, Miss Hamilton suggested everyone construct a carnival diorama over the weekend. On Monday, there were liquor boxes, shoe boxes, and even one refrigerator box filled with paintings, wire figurines, and paper mâché sculptures depicting lions, tigers, elephants, trapeze artists, clowns, and a black seal balancing a red striped ball on its nose. And then there was Theodore's contribution.

Theodore placed an old wooden matchbox on Miss Hamilton's desk. Inside was one piece of soiled sawdust, which he had collected from the stall of a neighbor's horse.

"What's this, Theodore?" asked his teacher.

"Smell."

Miss Hamilton leaned forward and inhaled deeply, wrinkling her nose at the pungent odor.

"It's the smell of the circus."

Years later at university, he pursued a dual major in sculpture and music and introduced himself simply as "T." He first entered into the public consciousness through music. His initial two concertos received warm critical reviews and modest enthusiasm from the public. The biggest consequence from these two pieces was that they drew the attention of Elvira Demitasse, a feisty, high-octane, sharp-elbowed, New York agent. Over the next year, T's music increasingly folded in on itself, and Elvira secured him ever-larger stages on which to shrink.

We all recognize the opening notes to Beethoven's Fifth Symphony—Da-Da-Da-DAH. Well, T, in his attempt at reductionism, wrote a symphony in which each movement contained a single, brief note. Elvira secured a rehearsal hall at Lincoln Center for its debut. The critics were stunned and in a good way. Who was this minimalist genius? The New York Times hailed T as the new John Cage, not so much for his approach to sound as for his audacity and the likely influence his musical breakthroughs would have on future generations of composers. Audiences were puzzled at first as they had expected a bit more for their two hundred dollar tickets, but they appreciated being able to get an early post-performance meal.

Encouraged, he pressed on. "Symphony," his next major musical achievement consisted of one chord drawn out over two hours, sort of like an Om on steroids. It, too, gained boffo reviews but drove the audience from the hall in screaming droves. In an attempt to reduce matters further, T created "S," a symphony of total silence. He filled Yankee Stadium, but the ambient city noises of sirens, screeching brakes, car alarms, foghorns from the Hudson, and rumblings from the subway, coupled with the coughing, snorting, shuffling, and sneezing of the audience, ruined the performance, a point driven home by his first unfavorable notices. He tried a second performance of "S"—this time barring any audience so as not to destroy the moment. Afterward, Elvira gently took him aside.

"You see, T, one of the conventions of a musical performance, even one absent of sound, sorta requires someone to listen to it, to say nothing of the economics of playing to an empty hall."

"Maybe we could put out a CD," T suggested.

"A CD of silence? Let me get back to you on that."

Abandoning music forever, T turned to the visual arts.

Feeling a need for an individual as well as an artistic transformation, it was at this time that T completed his final personal diminution by renaming himself simply, "t." With his new name, t was resigned to the fact that perfect minimalism was only for the gods, and for people, he would have to create something tangible.

His first breakthrough in the visual arts came with his series called One to Ten. In an otherwise vacant gallery, he placed ten, one-foot-high, sculpted numbers, all painted off-white. The critics were ecstatic. By the time the show moved from New York to Paris, t was down to just five numbers and had aptly renamed the display *Un à Cinq*. When the show reached San Francisco, it was simply "One" with the requisite adjustment to the display. The singular piece was received with worshipful enthusiasm and was scooped up in a moment of almost religious fervor by an aging film star for a mere $ 23 million.

Over the next few years, t's shows grew smaller and smaller, even as his successes grew larger. He was hailed as the Anti-Christo. As his pieces shrunk, his shows occurred less often, as if he were trying to match the frequency of his exhibits to their scale. As his agent and publicist, Elvira became increasingly exasperated. The smaller t's pieces became and the more infrequent his events, the bigger grew her responsibilities and challenges. Seeing perhaps the end to a remarkable career, Elvira suggested one more major effort.

"How 'bout a retrospective? We could call it simply 'Minimalism.' A lot of artists do that."

"You mean a room cluttered with three or four pieces." t shuddered, envisioning a gallery crowded with so much work. "No, I think we should do an exhibit entitled 'm,' and I have just the piece in mind."

Elvira managed to secure an empty warehouse in Tribeca. Over the next month, contractors cleaned the space and painted it white—walls, ceiling, floors, windows, doors, coat racks, everything.

On the night of the opening, the New York Art World descended on lower Manhattan. Stevie Wonder was there, talking up his new photography exhibit. The olfactory artist, Fragrancia, arrived with her odorous entourage. There were painters, sculptors, filmmakers, actors, writers, and agents. Marty, Bobby, Liza, Mikhail, Jerry, Woody, Whoopi, Bette were all in attendance. The Mayor showed up. Critics from every major newspaper and art magazine badgered Elvira to secure press passes. Patrons, investors, groupies, and hangers-on of every stripe elbowed their neighbors to grab a drink and jostled each other to secure a space from which they might be seen. Wine was spilled, canapés ground underfoot, the room resonated with air kisses and, "Dahlings."

In the center of the gallery was a white pedestal with a small object covered by a white silk cloth. At the appointed hour, t entered. A hush fell over the room. t walked up to the exhibit and removed the cloth. There, balanced on the head of a pin, was one, solitary grain of salt. Several overhead spotlights caught the sparkling edges of the crystal, refracting tiny beams of light and shining them over the heads of the onlookers.

With the crowd mesmerized by the dazzling display, t bent forward and, with a pair of tiny silver tweezers, picked up the particle of salt and, walking among the attendees, passed the salt under each and every nose. The sea. They smelled the sea, and they were transported back through their individual reveries to long ago days at the beach—seagulls, breezes, boardwalks, beach balls, tans, lemonade, taffy, morning jogs and evening strolls, sunrises and sunsets.

A new mother stood to one side with her infant held in her arms. t approached her and stroked the baby's cheek with the tiny piece of salt. The baby gurgled and, as the faintest of pink lines appeared on its snowy cheek, the viewers rested their hands on their own faces, perhaps recalling a mother's caress or a first kiss.

t picked up a small silver spoon and held it up to a microphone. He dropped the speck of salt on to the spoon. PING! The single note reverberated through the hollow warehouse. Heads turned as various amplifiers picked up the sound and bounced it from one wall to the next, at first becoming progressively louder then turning back in on itself and fading into the audible sighs of the assembled.

Carrying the spoon and its salt particle across the room, t stopped in front of a woman dressed in a white sheath, a single strand of pearls around her neck. She'd let her hair down for the night, and her silver-white mane settled on her porcelain shoulders. t lifted the spoon to her mouth. She parted her lips, and t placed the single speck of salt on her tongue, as if bestowing a communal blessing. Her mouth closed, as did her eyes. She tilted her face to the heavens. At this moment, when the sense of taste combined with the earlier sensations of sight, smell, touch, and sound, a single salty tear escaped from her eye and slid down her powdered cheek. From that solitary drop of salt water, an ocean of emotion engulfed the room in an explosive, startling, transitory, fading, vanished moment.

t gazed around the room at the silent spectators, some smiling, some crying, many on their knees. Elvira raced among the crowd collecting Visa cards in exchange for tiny ten-thousand-dollar commemorative boxes embossed with a miniscule "t" containing a single granule of salt. t walked from the room and stepped outside into the brisk night.

A sliver of moon shone alongside several stars. t looked up into the night sky framed by the towering granite and glass skyscrapers surrounding him. He felt small and comfortable and happy. Perhaps caught up in the moment and with the success of the evening, t wondered if there weren't further minimalist boundaries to pursue. He pulled the collar of his coat tightly around his neck and set off in search of a purveyor of microscopes.

The Lakeview Motel

When I returned to the brick rambler on Decatur Street, I expected old memories to greet me but not the past I found. After my father's death, Mom called my older sister and me home to triage the contents of the house: stuff to the dump, goods to donate, and a final, much smaller pile to sell on E-Bay. The rest Mom would take to Clayton, seven miles away, where she would go to live with her brother.

"Charlie, would you mind tackling Dad's closet?" Mom asked. "Maddie and I can take on my room."

Daddy's Girl shot me a bruised glance. As my sister was my father's clear favorite, why was I picked to go through his things? During the turbulent teenage years, she and Mom had brutal yelling matches, going days without speaking, but in my father's eyes she could do no wrong. During those same years, my father and I drifted apart, our relationship cordial but hardly warm. I took comfort from my mother leading Maddie to taunt me as the Momma's Boy. These family divisions help explain why Maddie and I were never close, but they don't account for the lengths we went to torment each other. I suspect the animosity had much to do with the secrets I now know we both harbored.

A few years earlier, my father had taken over the guest room, his restlessness at night interfering with Mom's sleep, or so they said. The morning sun slanted through the window, illuminating dust motes and the new absence suspended in the air and in our lives. I opened the closet door and ran my hand across the scratchy lapel of the gray tweed jacket my father wore on weekends. I got a whiff of the harsh smoke from the pipe tobacco he'd taken up after quitting cigarettes ten years earlier. His white dress shirts, starched and crisp as a curt reply, were still folded and taped with the thin bands of paper from the laundry. He never wore anything but a clean white shirt to his job at the bank.

After bagging his clothes for delivery to Goodwill, I turned to the upper shelves. From the highest shelf, I pulled down an old Florsheim shoebox, split along its seam and repaired with scotch tape, now yellowed. I sat down on the bed and opened the box. Inside, I found cracked photos of Christmases and Fourth of July picnics long past, a couple of silver fountain pens, and a small box holding two medals from the Vietnam War: a Purple Heart and an Army Commendation Medal. There was a black-handled, folding pocketknife, which I remembered him carrying and using to slit open bills and to peel apples. I slipped it into my pocket. At the bottom of the shoebox lay a travel brochure for the Lakeview Motel on Lake Erie.

I closed my eyes for a moment, the fragrance of pine trees enveloping me, and layered beneath that, something else moldy and rotten. I shook my head and looked down at the cover of the pamphlet. It had a colorized picture of the single-story motel, as it would have appeared when it first opened in the early 1950s. Fir trees towered over the twelve adjoining cabins. I turned the brochure over, and there was a picture of the beach leading down to the lake and the pier and the line of canoes and rowboats ready for rent. My stomach queased, and I wiped away the dampness on my forehead. I set the box down on the floor and lay back on the bed.

"What's wrong with you?" My sister stood at the door.

"Nothing," I said, sitting up. "Just taking a break."

She hesitated before proceeding down the hall.

It's nothing, I thought again. But, of course, it wasn't nothing.

In 1980 when I was six and had just finished kindergarten, my father took me up to Lake Erie for a week's fishing. We went every summer until I was eleven. We'd pack the car with jeans, flannel shirts, parkas, swimsuits, and rods and reels and bobbers. Mom would load in several bags of dry goods and a cooler filled with prepared meals for us to heat up. We planned on eating the fish we'd catch, but just in case, Mom wanted us fed. On the way north, as soon as we crossed the state line into New York, my father would stop at a roadside grocery. He'd wink at me, and we'd head over to the candy counter and fill a bag with Baby Ruths, Milky Ways, and Snickers. My father would also buy a case of Coke and a couple of bottles of Canadian Club. "Our little secret," he'd say, placing his finger to the side of his nose. We'd reach the Lakeview Motel by late afternoon, just in time to drop a line into the cool water under the rickety dock.

I'd often thought back to those days, the trips now a gauzy memory of flycatchers, tanagers, and warblers awakening the day; water glistening through the golden morning mist; wooden rowboats, their red paint chipped and peeling; the tell-tale plummeting of the cork plug and the jerk of the line; baloney or peanut butter sandwiches on white bread, compressed and soggy and delicious; dreamy afternoons filled with checkers, Go Fish, reading, and napping on the pine needles in the comforting shade of the fir trees along the bank of the lake.

As the sun slipped low in the sky, my father would open the small refrigerator in our room and retrieve a Coke. He'd pop the cap and pass it to me. He'd fill a glass with ice and pour himself a generous splash of the Canadian Club. As we drank, he'd fry up the fish we'd caught and heat up one of the dishes Mom had made, macaroni and cheese or lasagna, or he'd open a can and warm some beans or corn. We'd talk a bit about the day's adventures or simply sit in silence. With interest, I'd watch my father top up his drink with the amber liquid. At home, he only drank an occasional beer.

After the sun set, the breezes off the lake would fall, and the air would grow still, the evening filling with the sounds of crickets and owls and nightingales. I'd crawl into my bed and pull the musty sheet up to my neck. The mattress was lumpy and gave off a sour odor. I had remembered those days, but until I held the brochure in my hand, I'd forgotten the dark nights with their cloying dampness and the smell of rot rising through the floorboards and the howling of unseen creatures and the screaming of insects through the darkness. Soon, my father would drag one of the metal chairs outside, its legs scraping across the cracked concrete. Over the clink of ice in a glass, I'd hear the voices of women and bursts of laughter. To these sounds and to the smell of cigarette smoke and strange perfume drifting in through the window, I'd fall asleep. When I awoke at first light, my father would be in the next bed snoring softly. I'd get up and turn on the hot plate under the percolator, as he had shown me. Soon, to the smell of freshly brewing coffee, he'd stir, and another day at the lake would begin.

I noticed early on that the women in the cabin next to ours only stayed for a night or two, never accompanied by a husband or kids. In the early years, I paid this little mind, but as our summer visits to the lake went by, I found it odd, out of place.

During the summer when I was eleven, my unease grew. Then one night I awoke to find myself alone. There was no sound of laughter, or ice clinking, nor any smell of smoke or perfume. The only sound was the incessant buzzing and yelping out in the blackness, the only smell the mustiness that clung to everything

70

in the night. I got up and opened the front door. Two empty metal chairs rested against the wall, a tin ashtray overflowing with cigarette butts lying between them. Two sweating glasses sat on the windowsill of the adjoining cabin from which I heard a murmur. The curtain to the room had been pulled hastily, and a gap the width of my hand separated its two drapes. I placed my face to the screen. A bedside light illuminated my father lying naked on his back. A woman straddled him, my father cupping her large breasts in his hands. She rose and sank rhythmically above him, her eyes closed and her face tilted to the ceiling. I knew I shouldn't be seeing this, but I couldn't look away. As I shifted my hand on the windowsill, I knocked over one of the glasses. It tumbled to the walkway and shattered. My father snapped his head toward the window, and our eyes locked for a moment before I bolted and fled back to our room. The next morning, we packed up our gear and drove home. We never spoke of that night, and we never returned to the Lakeview Motel.

As the years passed, my recollection of those trips to the Lakeview Motel and our little secrets faded, leaving only glimpses of a small boy sitting in a rowboat or playing checkers and dining on fried bass and catfish and drinking sweet Cokes. The rest was forgotten or repressed. Until now.

I reached over and picked up the shoebox, and, as I slid the brochure for the Lakeview Motel into my pocket, Maddie entered the room.

"What's that?"

"A box of Dad's stuff. I found it on the top shelf of the closet."

She sat down next to me and fingered the items. "You didn't take anything, did you?"

"What?"

"I thought I saw you put something in your pocket as I was coming into the room."

"It's nothing," I said, removing the brochure and showing it to her. She took the pamphlet from me and turned it over. She shrugged and handed it back.

"Anything else?"

"Jesus, Maddie. Why are you this way? Do we really have to do this?" She just stared at me.

"Fine," I said and reached into my other pocket and took out the folding knife. "Just this. Just this old knife. It's nothing."

"You can't just help yourself to stuff. We need to discuss these things," she said, as she took the knife from my hand and opened the blade. "I gave this knife to him. I should have it."

"No, you didn't. He always had it."

"No, I gave it to him. It was for his birthday. You were too young to remember. It should be mine."

"Fine. Keep it. It's just an old knife."

She closed the blade and tossed it once into the air, catching it cleanly.

A week later, the house was packed. Maddie drove me to the airport, and, on the way, we stopped for lunch at Norma's Diner, where we'd each hung out in our high school days, drinking malts and eating hamburgers and listening to the latest hits on the old Wurlitzer.

As we were having coffee, my sister placed her hands around her cup, took a sip, and asked, "So, you going to tell me what's going on?"

"What do you mean?"

"Oh, come on, Charlie. You've been acting weird ever since you cleaned out Dad's closet. You're not pissed off about that knife, are you?"

I set aside a napkin I'd been shredding and leaned back in my chair. A part of me wanted my sister to preserve the myth of her father as perfect—the dutiful husband, the loving father, the honorable man. A less noble part wanted to show her that the man she considered to be such a paragon was deeply flawed. For whatever reasons, and for probably the wrong ones, I decided she had a right to the truth. Yet, I gave her one more chance. "Sure, you want to know?"

She looked at me for a moment, perhaps sensing a door about to open she might prefer sealed. Then she nodded and said, "Give."

So, I told the story of my six summers at the Lakeview Motel. I could see the change in her eyes as she rewrote her own history, and I could almost see the cracks appear and spread in the iconic portrait she had created over the years of my father. I also realized, too late, there was nothing in my telling that would redeem me in her eyes or gain the sympathy I longed for. Rather, I could see we would drift further apart in the years ahead, as she would never forgive me for the telling of the tale and its consequences for her own story.

"I think we better head for the airport," I said.

She looked at her watch. "We've got time for one more cup."

We sat in silence for a couple of minutes until the tension in the air led me to ask, "So?"

"So," she said, as the waitress turned away from topping up our coffees. Maddie looked at me and, apparently reaching a decision, tried to smile but failed. Instead, she tilted her head to one side and asked, "Ever wonder what Mom did while you and Dad were off fishing?"

A Night at the Taj

I n 1960, things were decidedly more lax for a boy of fifteen. Then, I lived in India while my father worked for the United Nations. During the three years we lived there, my parents gave me an amazing degree of freedom to explore my new home, a degree of freedom unimaginable today in the United States, to say nothing of more exotic locations.

Even so, when my friend Van said, "Why don't we go to Agra and spend the night to see the Taj Mahal?" I responded, "Just the two of us? My parents will never let me do that." But they did.

The September morning of our departure was hot. The monsoon season had just ended, but its humidity lingered.

When the conductor opened the gate for the Delhi-Agra Express and yelled, "Sub Charo!" Van and I surged forward with the waiting throng to battle for the few seats in the third-class compartment, those being the only seats our limited budget would permit. The more experienced travelers knew what to do. Some bypassed the crowded and overheated compartments and climbed up the ladders at the ends of the railway cars to make the journey on the roof of the train. This was more excitement than we dared. Others clambered through the open windows while we headed for the compartment door. By the time we wrestled aboard, the only space available was on the grimy floor by the train's open door, only a few feet away from the foul-smelling lavatory.

As the steam locomotive slammed into the waiting cars, lurching them forward, an itinerant Hindu holy man, a Sadhu, raced across the platform and extended his arm for an assist to board the moving train. I reached out and grabbed his hand, and he tumbled across us as the train pulled out of the station.

Nodding and smiling, he settled in next to us on the floor. He sat cross-legged, and his bony, brown knees protruded from his dusty, saffron robes. He had a scraggly beard, and his hair was long and matted. A tilak, a white and red mark was smeared across his forehead, symbolizing his sect and piety.

The train hurtled along, jostling us from side to side through the open plains of Uttar Pradesh. The wind blew through the door tousling our hair, cooling us down. Van reached into his pocket and pulled out a pack of cheap, unfiltered Panama cigarettes. As we lit up, the Sadhu gestured that he would appreciate a smoke. He acknowledged the cigarette with a slight Namaste and a laugh. "Shukrya," he said.

"Bahuta Accha."

I smiled, his meaning being clear enough. He smoked the cigarette down to its last inch, popped the smoldering butt into his mouth, chewed it up, and swallowed.

We'd planned our visit so that after we had a chance to explore the city, we'd arrived at the Taj at eight in the evening, an hour before the gates closed. We'd planned our visit to coincide with the full moon rising over the timeless mausoleum.

But back then, seeing the Taj under the moonlight was the highlight to any trip to India. Unfortunately, these days, the Indian Government restricts access to the Taj at night and turns off all illumination due to security concerns. In this post 9/11-world, India has its own threats to deal with, whether from Pakistan or China or from internal groups that fuel violence between Hindus, Sikhs, and Moslems. Like the Twin Towers, the Taj Mahal is a prominent target, but back then, rather than being scrutinized at the entrance by heavily armed police and bag checks, only a single sleepy ticket taker and a slouching watchman armed with a bamboo pole greeted us.

It was a mild night with soft warm breezes, and we explored the shrine and the lush and fragrant gardens in silence, struck by the peace and serenity in such sharp contrast to the bustling city just outside the gates.

As it came time to leave, we found ourselves in a secluded corner protected from view by a four-foot hedge. The lawn was lush and still warm from the day's earlier light, the scent of freshly cut grass filling the air.

"Why don't we just sleep here tonight?" Van said.

"Here? You mean at the Taj?"

"Yeah. We don't have a hostel room yet. It's warm. The grass is soft. We can save a few rupees. We'll leave in the morning and catch the train back to Delhi as we planned. It'll be fun."

"They'll never let us stay here."

"Shit, everything's so loosey-goosey. We had to wake up the ticket taker when we came in. He's probably sound asleep again. They don't know whether we're still here or not."

With that, we heard someone calling out from the vicinity of the gate. "Bund Ka Rho Hai. Bund Ka Rho Hai."

"I think maybe they know we're still here," I said.

"Well, so what?" said Van. "They've got to find us in the dark, and if they do, we'll just tell them we didn't realize that the place closed, and all we were doing was watching the Taj in the moonlight. That's what everyone talks about, right? The Taj in the moonlight. What's the worst that can happen?"

So that's what we did—spent the night at the Taj Mahal.

Periodically, I got up to watch the shrine as the moon moved across the sky until it set to be replaced by a night full of stars. I could hear the traffic, music, and bustle of the city in the distance, but they were only a faint din, overpowered by the rustling of the leaves stirred by the soft breezes and by the chirping of crickets. The air smelled clean, freshened by the cool water in the Taj's reflecting pools. I imagined that it must have been on nights like this more than three hundred years earlier when Shah Jahan roamed these same gardens and looked upon the monument he had built to celebrate his love for Mumtaz Mahal, his mourned for wife.

Eventually, I heard birds singing and dogs barking in the distance, and a pink glow emerged in the east. The air became pungent with smoke from the early morning dung fires brewing chai and warming chapattis. Van and I watched the sun rise over the mausoleum in this early stillness, the light slowly brightening and changing the hue of the minarets and the dome from pink to red to ochre to saffron to gold to silver and finally to a dazzling white.

With the morning upon us, we were hungry and ready to leave, but caution dictated that we delay our departure until the morning's visitors arrived and gave us cover. We kept out of sight until the gates opened and a few tour groups filtered into the garden. We mingled in with these early visitors and, after a suitable period, made our way to the exit.

As we crossed the threshold, an angry guard carrying a bamboo stick stormed out of an office. "Idir Ana Mana Hai." Someone had noticed us after all. "Idir Ana Mana Hai," he yelled again.

While spittle flew from his betel nut-stained mouth, we feigned ignorance, shrugging our shoulders and claiming we didn't understand. "Idir Ruko," he said, pointing at us and then at the ground, indicating we were to stay put while he found someone in authority to bridge the language barrier.

When he stepped back into his office, Van and I looked at each other, nodded, and made a mad dash down the street away from the Taj. We heard yelling but didn't look back as we turned the corner, running another couple of blocks before slowing down and mixing in with the morning shoppers. After more detours up and down side streets, we began to relax. Then, we were laughing. People walking alongside us on the street smiled.

"What would they have done to us?" I asked.

"Who knows?" Van said. "Probably yelled a lot. Maybe called our parents. At worst, our folks might have had to come down and spread around a little baksheesh."

And Van was probably right. That likely would have been the extent of it in those years so far removed from today's world of armed guards and metal detectors and suicide bombers and exploding cars and trucks: a world where children are kept indoors or restricted to supervised play dates rather than encouraged to run free; a world where they lock the gates to the Taj Mahal at sunset.

The Fatalist

"*Un café, s'il vous plait*," you say.

"*Certainement, monsieur. Immediatement.*"

You're sitting at a small circular table with a black and white marble top outside Bistro Michel on Boulevard Saint-Germain. You've come to Paris after completing five days of intense negotiations in Istanbul, sales meetings involving hundreds of millions of dollars of aerospace equipment exports to Turkey. The talks were successful, your boss indicating pleasant things for your career on your return to Chicago. He even suggested you take the long weekend in Paris to unwind—all on the company, of course. And so, before leaving Istanbul, you called home to Beverly.

"So, it sounds as if things went very well," Bev says.

"Better than very well. I came up with the strategy that broke the logjam. Trevor was quite impressed."

"I'll bet. Congratulations."

"Yeah, so anyway, he's suggested I stop off in Paris for the long weekend. Stay at the company's apartment, all expenses paid. How about flying over?"

"Oh, man, I'd love to. Paris, wow, but I can't. I'm hosting the luncheon for the Junior Chamber. There's no way I can get someone else to step in at this point. But you should go."

"By myself?"

"Sure. You don't want to turn down Trevor's hospitality. Enjoy. It's only for the weekend. I'll be fine, and it sounds like there will be other, future opportunities. I'm so proud of you. Take advantage of this unexpected chance."

So, you changed your flights and now find yourself sipping your espresso and watching the stylish French women dressed to the nines promenade down the sidewalk. Who would have thought last week in Chicago you'd be spending this weekend in Paris? Not you, but, on the other hand, you do appreciate life is full of unexpected turns.

"I'm a fatalist," you often comment. You aren't troubled by the idea that surprises occur, both opportunities and setbacks. You don't anguish over the fact bad things happened to good people or good things to bad people. You don't believe in Karma or Predestination, but you do appreciate 'Shit Happens'. It just happens haphazardly; sometimes it's good, sometimes bad. Oh sure, you understand you have some control over your fate; smoke too much and you'll get lung cancer, drink too much and your liver will conk out. It isn't that you're irresponsible, but rather you feel you can only do so much. You gotta go with the flow. Regardless of how conscientious you are, there are things out there waiting to alter your plans: Good things like bumping into the beautiful woman at the produce counter who will become your wife, conducting successful negotiations leading to promotions, getting all expense paid weekends in Paris; and bad things like drunk drivers about to cross centerlines, ladders with loose rungs, yogurts with a few too many active cultures, homicidal terrorists with AK-47s and grudges.

But the funny thing is, though you accept all this intellectually, somehow, you never think the bad things will actually happen to you. You're sort of like people of faith, who, though they believe in Hell, don't think they'll be the ones going there, regardless of their misdeeds. You think you're headed for Heaven or, at least, the occasional weekend in an exotic city.

And now you are sitting in Paris enjoying the late afternoon, sipping your coffee, while at that very moment, unbeknownst to you, your boss Trevor has your beautiful wife's ankles interlaced around his neck. If you return to Chicago in two days, you'll find your wife asking for a divorce, your job at the aerospace firm gone, your bed for the night in a Quality Inn on North Martingale, and you will forget your comfort with fatalism and instead be wondering 'What the Fuck?' But you may not be returning to Chicago. Thirty-five minutes earlier, Jean-Claude Duvalier, a journalist with Le Monde, got behind the wheel of his two-year old, light blue Renault after a long lunch with friends involving too many bottles of Beaujolais.

You take another sip of coffee and think once again about your triumph in Istanbul, how you had buttonholed the Turkish Head of Delegation in the Men's Room and quietly suggested he request the substitution of the newer version of avionics, all at the same price. That became the key modification to the contract that aced the deal. But not speaking Turkish, you didn't understand it when the Turkish Head of Delegation turned to his aide and said, "Who is this asshole?" Nor did you see the fury behind Trevor's eyes when he realized you had subverted his authority by speaking directly to the Turks rather than presenting your idea to him. What you saw as initiative, the Turkish Head of Delegation saw as impertinence. What you saw as resourcefulness, Trevor saw as disloyalty.

As you continue to bask in your moment of imagined glory in the late afternoon of this fine October day on this busy Parisian street, the drunken Jean-Claude Duvalier turns left on Rue De Richelieu, clipping the curb and startling the two elderly ladies walking their dogs. He'll next turn on to Boulevard Saint-Germain and within six minutes hit a pothole and swerve in front of the Bistro Michel. He'll lose control of his Renault, the car veering across the sidewalk, destroying the very table and chair where you now sit.

You look at your watch and see you have time for another espresso before returning to the apartment to shower and dress for dinner with your old college friend from the American Embassy. Or you could leave now and meander over to the Champs-Élysées and stroll up to the Arch de Triomphe. It's a beautiful evening for a leisurely walk.

"Garçon," you say, catching your waiter's eye, while Jean-Claude Duvalier barrels down the Boulevard Saint-Germain three minutes from his rendezvous at the Bistro Michel.

"*Un autre café, monsieur, ou l'addition?*" asks the waiter.

Poaching

Jesse Doyle was born trouble.

You don't have to take my word for it; even his own momma said so in her more lucid moments. The other four kids had just popped right out on the bed they'd been conceived in. No problem. No real need for Doc Jackson though it was a comfort to have him there with his confident smile and sure hands. But Jesse, now that was different. Took a night of screaming and sweating and blood-soaked sheets and a last-minute dash down the frozen roads to the new hospital all the way over in Roanoke to bring him into the world. Even the next day, it looked iffy for both mother and child from the loss of all that blood. They pulled through, but his momma was never the same—something to do with a loss of oxygen. She was still there, but she wasn't, if you know what I mean. And Jesse? Trouble ever after. Everyone said so.

My name is Webb. I was born in these Blue Ridge Mountains in 1900, more than fifty years ago, four days after the start of the new century. Lived here all my life, except for three years in the Pacific, jumping from one steamy island to the next, killing Japs and trying not to get killed in return. But this is not my story, it's Jesse's. Since he's not here to tell it, I guess it falls to me. And that's fair enough. Though the cost of what happened was graver for him, I wasn't unaffected.

I'd shot a buck at dawn, gutted him, and hung him in my barn. I'd skin and butcher him in two or three days. Stripping off my bloody overalls and washing the gore from my hands under the spigot next to the chicken hutch, I could look over the ravine to the neighboring hill. Smoke drifted through the tops of the white pines, red oaks, and tulip poplars like morning mist lifting off a still pond. Though I couldn't see the small log and stone house obscured by the thick August growth, I knew the smoke rose from the chimney of the Doyle's cabin where eggs, bacon, and biscuits were cooking on the old cast iron kitchen stove, the cabin where Jesse used to live.

The Doyles lived simply enough, and it was a happy home by most accounts, until Jesse arrived. Hard working, plain speaking, church going, help-your-neighbor kind of people. Maybe it could have continued that way, even considering the way Jesse's momma was. Trouble started early when Jesse was just crawling. Things got broken, even the crystal bud vase with the silver band that belonged to Pop Doyle's great-grandmother that had been put high up on the sideboard out of harm's way. Shattered. Smashed to smithereens on the floor, and a shard of glass embedded so deep in Jesse's pudgy knee that Pop had to pull it out with a pair of needle-nose pliers and stitch the wound closed with a darning needle and button thread, leaving a knobby, pink scar.

I'd grown up with Pop Doyle. You'd think he got his nickname from one of his five children, but the truth was he was called Pop as a kid himself. He had a fondness for Dr. Pepper—close to addiction. All his after-school earnings from stocking the shelves at Cleary's Hardware went into soda. He'd rather be holding a bottle of pop than the hand of a young girl, so that's how he spent his money—soda pop—rather than on tickets to the movie show over in New Castle or on bottles of Vitalis hair tonic like the rest of us. And that's how he got the nickname and may explain why he wed late in these parts, not having much experience with the opposite sex. After he was married, though, he made up for lost time, and each of his five kids was only a year apart. He might've had more, but Jesse put an end to that.

All those kids running around underfoot may explain how on some evenings Pop'd wander over to my place to sit a spell and enjoy a smoke. I think he liked my company, but I know he liked the quiet. Having lost my young wife, she died during the flu epidemic back in 1919, the one thing I had in abundance was peace and quiet and lots of it. Sometimes Pop'd tell me about his puzzlement over Jesse and try to fathom why he was so different from the rest of them. Pop doesn't come to visit anymore, but that's not surprising considering all that's happened.

When Jesse could actually walk, matters went further downhill. Things started going missing. Not just the odd sock or spoon or the Jack of Clubs from the good deck of cards. Not things you'd expect to get lost and not give a second thought to. No, things like the handle off the outhouse door, the knob off the dresser, the plug off the lamp, the number nine from the route number on the mailbox. Things screwed down tight. Things nailed shut. Bits and pieces that should have outlasted us all. Turn around, and they were gone.

When Jesse got older and went off to school and was more on his own, stuff got stolen. Not lost, not missing, not misplaced, but taken. Taken deliberately. Some old, trashy, plastic beads his Aunt Florence brought back from New Orleans—stolen right out of the white porcelain bowl she kept on the side table near her front door; the one where she stacked her mail and tossed her keys. The flag from in front of the junior high school, taken clean off the pole in broad daylight. His sister Beth's rhinestone necklace, the neighbor's silver wind chime, his mother's compact—the gold one with the mirror inside, all taken. For a while, it seemed as if nothing sparkly or shiny was safe from the boy. And he was clever. You'd rarely catch him with the goods. But you knew. There just wasn't any other explanation.

Pop told me on one of his nighttime visits he'd confronted Jesse after finding the gold compact hidden under the boy's mattress.

"Jesse, why'd you steal your momma's compact? You know it's wrong."

"I was just keeping it safe. Momma gave it to me."

"She says she didn't."

"She just don't remember. You know how she is."

"What were you going to do with a woman's compact?"

"I need the mirror for a science project at school. I was going to give it back. Ask Momma."

Seemed like whenever he got caught doing something he shouldn't, he'd smile that smile of his and tilt his head a bit to the side and charm himself right out of trouble again. By high school, he was handsome. A dimple on his right cheek that lit up whenever he grinned. The bluest eyes you ever saw, more startling for being set in that dark face under that head of black hair. When the sunlight hit them…, well most of the girls in Craig County had a crush on him, including Mattie Harper.

The Harpers ran the dairy down in the bottomland just below my property line. It was rich, dark soil, and the grass grew thick and lush. About thirty to forty cows would be my guess. They made a good living and bought a new Chevy every three or four years—a sedan, not very practical but nice. But Lord, cows are hard work. Everyone in the family had to pitch in from morning till night. Mattie was their third child but the first girl. From the time she could walk, she was expected to pull her weight. She grew into a striking young lady—solid but feminine. She had curly, brown hair and green eyes and a figure that you couldn't help but notice. It wasn't an easy life, but she wasn't known as a complainer, and she seemed to flourish.

For a while, Mattie came to work for me. I can take care of myself pretty good, but I'll be the first to admit my place benefited from the hand of a woman. Mattie would stop by on her way home from school Mondays and Thursdays. She'd spend a couple of hours doing chores—washing, cleaning, and sometimes preparing a meal. I could manage these things myself, but she needed the money, and I enjoyed the company. More often than not, we'd share a cup of coffee and a piece of pie around the kitchen table. She'd tell me a little bit about her day at school, and leaning back in the hickory chair built by my grandfather, I'd offer some advice or tell her how it was when I was in school, or maybe I'd just listen. Sometimes I'd surprise her with a special gift, ribbons for her hair or a new comb and brush set. For her birthday, I got her some perfume, the real stuff from Paris, France. Each Monday and Thursday afternoon, she'd dependably arrive like a warm spring breeze.

Until Jesse came sniffing around.

Maybe it was his difficult birth or the mother that was there but not really. Maybe it was because Jesse was the youngest child, maybe it was the star he was born under, maybe it was just how it was supposed to be. Who can account for these things? But it was hard to see him as a Doyle. Pop was a stonemason. Build you the finest, strongest, straightest chimney you ever saw. Your whole house could burn to the ground taking with it everything you cared about, and you'd want to rebuild on that exact same spot just so you could fit in the old chimney and fireplace… happened more than once.

And the two older boys worked right alongside Pop, passing him just the right stone, working from morning to night. Give Pop and his boys credit; you hired them, you got your money's worth and then some. And Jesse's two sisters? Mary married and moved up to Albemarle County. Married well to a teacher, I heard. And Beth, just as pretty and well-mannered as a girl could be. People puzzled how Jesse could be kin to these fine folks.

"You don't watch that boy, you all going to have a regular juvenile delinquent on your hands. Mark my words," said Preacher Abbott on more than one occasion. "Just mark my words."

By seventeen, he was running wild, had little time for school, spent his days in the hills doing God knows what. Poaching most likely, judging from the rifle reports echoing through the trees out of season. Prize fruits and vegetables went missing from gardens. Pies were filched off windowsills before they had a chance to cool. One day, Paul Taylor's new overalls went missing off the clothesline. The next day, someone, I think it was Delores McBride, if I remember rightly, swore she saw Jesse strolling down Cumberland Lane without a care in the world with that rifle of his laying easily across his shoulder and him sporting a new set of denims rolled up at the ankles so they wouldn't drag in the dirt.

Even at seventeen, people gave him a wide berth. He was unpredictable. You could lecture him all day on the value of hard work and the need to apply himself, and he'd nod like he was taking it all in and then disappear into the hills, skipping three days of school in a row. You could call him a thieving liar to his face, and he seemed to take no offense. He'd just tilt his head to the side and favor you with that dimpled grin of his and look like goodwill incarnate. Another time you'd just give him a simple piece of advice, and he'd fly off the handle like that time at the counter in Clapper's Diner.

I was having breakfast that morning when he walked in, nodded, and sat two stools down.

"Jesse, your hat," I said.

He ignored me, his face buried in the menu.

"Jesse, Pop brought you up better than that. Take off your hat when you're inside, especially at the table."

Silence.

"Don't ignore me, boy. Take off your hat before—"

"Before what, old man?" he said, putting down the menu and swiveling on the stool toward me.

Before I gave it much thought, I was off my stool and moving toward him. He stood, and in one fluid motion picked up the chrome napkin holder and bounced it off my head yelling, "Don't you touch me. Nobody touches me."

He looked around at the other customers, all frozen in their seats from a combination of disbelief and fear. Then he walked to the door and out into the morning, strolling up Main Street as if he hadn't a care in the world. A thin trickle of blood ran down my forehead and into my left eye. I sat back down and placed a wad of napkins to my brow.

The sheriff came by when he heard about the fuss. I never cared much for Sheriff Colton. He has a feral look about him, his beady eyes focused off into the distance with that mixture of ignorance and arrogance you see too often in the eyes of rural cops. I wasn't about to hand him Jesse. Maybe it was because of Pop. Maybe I didn't like someone else fighting my battles. Anyway, my point was Jesse could be unpredictable, like I said.

But, to give him his due, he could also be surprisingly kind.

When Bill Slater was laid up with black lung, Marge came out of the house one day to find three cords of wood cut and stacked along the side of the house. Someone said they'd seen Jesse heading out earlier with his saw, ax, and maul. When Tucker, Will Stuart's pointer, went missing, Jesse showed up the next morning with the dog in his arms. Carried it down from Hodge's Mountain where it had got snake bit. And old Mrs. Caruthers always told of the venison Jesse brought after her operation, the meat all trimmed and cubed and ready for stewing.

But most people remember him as trouble.

"Kids will be kids," some would say. A stupid saying to my mind, usually said by parents too lazy or too ignorant to lay down the law, but for whatever reason, folks gave Jesse leeway as well as a wide berth.

Soon after Jesse began to hang around Mattie, she started missing her afternoons at my place. When she did show up, she'd be sullen, and our conversations became awkward. Soon she stopped coming altogether. I missed her company. Coffee and pie just don't taste the same when they aren't shared. I heard that her grades suffered, and there were disciplinary problems at school. Her parents punished her more than once, but it didn't do any good. I saw Mattie myself sneaking out of my barn, which was about a quarter mile up the lane from the Harper place, and on close examination later, I'd seen the depression in the warm hay up in the loft and the stubs from the Camels Jesse was known to smoke. I asked him about the cigarettes when I ran into him walking on the road to town. He had two rabbits slung over his shoulder and a .22 cradled in the crook of his arm.

"Jesse, I found some Camel butts up in my loft."

"And you think they're mine?"

"It crossed my mind," I said, my thumb coming up to the small scar on my brow over my right eye.

"Why do you always give me such a hard time, Mr. Webb?" He put his hands in his back pockets and tilted his head to the side.

"I don't always give you a hard time. I just asked a question. A simple question."

He pursed his lips and nodded. "It doesn't have anything to do with Mattie, does it?" he asked.

"What's that supposed to mean?"

"Well, Mattie told me how you used to always get yourself all gussied up when she came over to do chores for you. Slicking your hair back, putting on a clean shirt, giving her French perfume, and smiling at her. Looking her up and down."

"That's enough."

"An old guy like you. Pretty stupid to think a young girl would think you were anything but ridiculous."

"Mind yourself, Jesse. You're way out of line."

He looked at me for a moment, squinting his blue eyes against the glare of the sun. He shifted the rifle laying the barrel against his shoulder so that it pointed up into the trees. Then he nodded and smiled. "You're right. I apologize. And, 'No,' I didn't smoke any cigarettes up in your loft. I know better than to smoke in a hayloft, even when the hay's still damp. What would I be doing up there anyway?"

Things seemed to go from bad to worse. Mattie's folks had enough and decided at the end of the school term they'd send the girl off to an aunt's in Charlottesville for the summer. The aunt had gotten her some kind of a job in the library of the university.

The evening Mattie went missing, word of her disappearance blazed through the county. I was in Cleary's Hardware Store when I heard about it for the fourth or fifth time. I was there buying some bailing wire, chicken feed, and a box of double-ought shotgun shells. I'd been having trouble with a fox getting into the hen house, and while the double-oughts were overkill, I was determined to give myself every advantage in dealing with the varmint.

"Webb, did you hear about the Harper girl gone a missing?"

"Yeah, I heard. Probably just lost track of the time."

"But she was supposed to go home right after school for a fitting of the dress. She's to be in Samantha's wedding, you know."

"That right?"

"Her folks are calling everyone. Been down by the pond, too."

"Look, kids are always losing track of the time. We all need to take a deep breath."

"But missing the fitting and all. Something ain't right."

"We'll see."

"Guess that's right. No news is good news." Another of the stupid things people say if you ask me. I doubt the Harpers thought no news of their missing daughter was a good thing. Truth was, I didn't see anything good about it either.

Just then, in walked Jesse calm as could be with blood on his overalls—and not just a little blood. Cleary spoke up from behind the counter.

"What you been up to, Jesse?" he asked. "Where'd all that blood come from?"

"This here blood? Shoot, it's old from when Pop and I slaughtered a hog."

But to me, the blood looked fresh, and anyway, it was the wrong time of year to be putting up hams and rendering soap.

"You hear anything about Mattie?" I asked. "Folks say she's gone missing."

"Mattie? Why you so interested in Mattie, Mr. Webb?"

Sam Tyler got up in his face. "Don't you be so high and mighty, young fella," he said, poking at Jesse's shoulder with his gnarled finger.

Jesse pushed right by old Tyler, shoving him aside, and was out the door before anyone had the wits to grab him.

"I'm calling the Sheriff," Cleary said, walking over to the wall and cranking the box.

"Let's not get ahead of ourselves," I said. "We all know Jesse wouldn't hurt Mattie."

"Maybe not, but I'm calling anyhow."

"Well, let me know if you hear anything. If she's still missing at bedtime, I'll help with the search party," I said, gathering up my purchases.

It was a couple of hours later when I heard the ruckus. I'd finished my dinner of pork and beans and dark bread and set my dishes in the sink to soak. I was sitting on the porch smoking my evening pipe, watching the moon rise over the tree line behind the Doyle's' place when I heard a thud in the barn. Sounded like something tipped over or fell from a shelf, landing heavily on the floor. I thought of the fox going after more of my chickens, and I grabbed my shotgun from behind the door as I made my way to the barn. I didn't have any real hope of getting off a shot. The noise in the barn would have been enough to send him scampering back to his den. The sumbitch had dodged me more times than I liked to recall, leaving behind a trail of feathers and entrails. But I'd feel more a fool if I came face to face with the varmint and didn't have my gun. I don't know why I didn't think about Jesse.

I came upon the boy climbing down from the loft. I don't know who was more surprised. I don't believe he would have done me real harm. Now, I think he only swung the rifle toward me trying to secure his grip on the ladder while balancing the bundle he held under his arm. I shot him in the leg. It was just a reflex on my part. I didn't even aim or nothing. It just happened. The force of the blast of buckshot kicked his leg out from under him and clear off the ladder's rung, and he lost his footing and fell to the hard-packed earthen floor, breaking his fool neck. The blood from the hole in his leg seeped into the dirt beneath him.

Killing a boy is a terrible thing no matter how justified. Even a boy like Jesse Doyle. It opens a hole in you that can't easily be filled. You think about all the possibilities simply set aside. The waste. You note your many years and set them against his reduced tally. It doesn't matter much that everyone saw it coming from his earliest years. "That boy was born trouble," everyone said it. But still.

I stood over him for a few minutes that night. There wasn't any question he was dead, the way his neck jutted to the left. Nothing alive could hold itself in such a position. He didn't look like he'd suffered any pain. Instantaneous is what the coroner later said. Whether from the surprise or some other reason, Jesse seemed to be smiling up at me from the floor. His head tilted to the side and the dimple on his right cheek caught the moonlight streaming in from the transom. I stepped away from him and went into the house to call the sheriff.

The sheriff ruled it an accidental shooting though I could tell by the narrow way he regarded me from under the brim of his hat, he thought me a damn fool for getting startled by the boy, but because Jesse was carrying his deer rifle and was trespassing on my property, no one was going to make an issue out of it.

It turned out Jesse'd been up in my hayloft retrieving some clothes and money he'd hidden up there. As weeks went on, others found caches of food, clothing, and money on their places. Looked like he knew there'd eventually come a day of reckoning.

And Mattie? They found her later that night in front of Jesse's tent high up on Hodge's Mountain sitting cross-legged on a worn tarp and pressing a shiny gold compact between her palms. An out-of-season doe hung upside down from a nearby tree, it's throat slit to drain the blood. A haunch of fresh venison was roasting over a glowing fire.

Ash Wednesday

He'd walked over to Calliope Street from his apartment next to the Orpheum Theatre. He'd boarded the streetcar heading uptown for his morning amble through Audubon Park. The melody from "Here Comes the Sun King," was looping through his head when he turned the corner on the path near the river and the snare of her cigarette's smoke snagged his gaze.

She sat on a bench, her features hard to discern in the mottled shadows of the swaying branches of the Live Oaks. She leaned forward, her red shirt flaring for a moment like an ember in the night of a dying fire. Resting her forearms on her thighs, her coal black hair haloed her bent head, her eyes cast down at the ground, perhaps examining a distant memory or maybe simply the cigarette held in her left hand. Ash fell from the cigarette's tip, the gray cylinder tumbling in the slight morning breeze, settling on the ground. She toed the ash with her right boot, turning it to dust. Hearing his tread on the gravel, she looked up but didn't see him as he was invisible, as graying men in their fifties are to young girls just flirting with twenty.

Maureen would have been her age, but Maureen had drowned on a last day of summer when she was four. His thoughts had drifted on that afternoon by Lake Pontchartrain, and when he looked back, Maureen had vanished. They'd cremated the remains, so slight the ashes barely dusted the bottom of the urn. They cast them on the Mississippi, a gentle waft of air picking up a few errant flakes and marking the rocks at their feet with a Lenten blessing.

Unlike today's warm, breezy morning, then it had been cold and largely still, a gauzy mist rising from the muddy water, smelling of rot and chemicals and salt from the sea pushed up river by the tides from the Gulf. He'd rubbed the dampness from his face.

Now, as he continued his walk, he heard a child's laughter, and he stopped to let it peal. He entertained the conceit that if he could be patient a moment longer, the sound might take form and burst into this new day's light. But once again, he weakened and gazed behind to find a soundless and empty bench, on the pavement before it a smudge of ash being erased by the morning's breath.

A New York Moment

As we step from the East Village's Punjabi Restaurant, the scent of cumin, cardamom, and coriander follow us into the damp city evening. A late spring shower has washed the street clean, and the red, green, and yellow reflections from the traffic lights and neon signs bounce off the glistening black pavement. A yellow taxi pulls up to the curb in front of the restaurant, dislodging a young couple.

"Where to?" asks the cab driver, turning over the meter as we settle into the rear seat.

We give an address over on the West Side. Pulling into the traffic, our cabbie resumes talking into his cell phone in a language I can't understand yet sounds familiar. Years earlier, when I grew up in New York, cab drivers were from Brooklyn or the Bronx and gave their opinions in accents laced with "Dems, Dees, and Dos." Today's drivers are more likely to come from Calcutta, Mogadishu, or Tehran, speaking with their own unique accents.

Even in the light rain, the streets are full of couples, young and old, laughing and talking. In 2010, this is the new New York—clean, optimistic, safe. People are out and about looking for excitement and enjoying each other's company. Not that everything is perfect. As we cross Broadway, we look south to the lighted up construction site where the Twin Towers once stood.

"Are you visiting the city?" our driver asks.

"Yes, we're here for the weekend."

"And from where do you come?"

"From Annapolis."

My wife adds, "It's in Maryland. It's the capital of the state."

"I've heard of Annapolis. It's near Washington, DC, isn't it?"

"Yes, you're quite right."

My wife and I have flown up for the weekend. The short flight was predictably miserable with all the necessary but inconvenient added security. I look at the taxicab license displayed next to the meter. Malik Junaid Ahmed.

"And where are you from?" I ask.

He pauses before quietly saying, "Pakistan."

A week earlier, Faisal Shahzad, a newly minted American from Pakistan tried to set off a bomb in Times Square only a few blocks north. Our driver glances back at us in the rearview mirror before returning his gaze to the street. A silence fills the cab. My wife shifts in her seat. I stare out the window, no longer seeing the passing crowds but thrust back a half century in time.

"I've been there," I say.

"You have been to Pakistan?"

"I lived in India as a teenager, in Delhi. My father worked with the United Nations. In the spring of 1961, we drove from Delhi to Kabul and back, driving back and forth across Pakistan. We crossed into Pakistan at Lahore, then on to Rawalpindi and Peshawar, and through the Northwest Territories to the Khyber Pass, and on into Afghanistan."

"You have been to Lahore? That is my home. Actually, I lived in a small town called Mari. Have you ever heard of it?"

"No, I haven't."

"Well, it is very small. I went to school in Lahore. My wife and small daughter live there now. I hope to bring them over to the U.S. soon."

"It must be hard to be separated from them."

"Very hard. But sometimes one must make sacrifices."

At Fifth Avenue and Washington Square, traffic comes to a standstill. Ahead, the entrance to the park is aglow from the flashing lights from several emergency vehicles. We crane our necks trying to see what has disturbed the night. A policeman directs us to a detour on Eighth Street.

As traffic picks up again, our driver asks, "So, how did you find Pakistan?"

"I found it welcoming. Wherever we went, people opened their homes to us and treated us with great affection and respect. Parts of the country were very beautiful. I remember heading up into the mountains and seeing the Hindu Kush range for the first time. It was spectacular."

"Did you enjoy the food?"

"Of course. The freshly baked naan, the spicy chicken tikka, the succulent lamb kebabs, or maybe they were goat."

"Ha, yes, yes. Sometimes they will serve you goat and call it lamb, but delicious anyway, isn't it?"

"Yes, it is."

A panel truck swerves in front of us. Our driver curses words I can't understand while breaking and honking his horn. The truck makes a right turn, and we proceed south down Seventh Avenue.

"Do you have family over here?" I ask.

"My father lives in New Jersey with one of my brothers. My brother works for my father. They have an import/export business, but things are slow. I take night courses at City College in management. I hope to join them in the business soon. Do you think taking management courses is a good use of my time?"

"I think education is good. It sounds like you have a good plan. I wish you luck."

"Thank you. Yes, I think it is a good plan, too."

We pull up in front of the apartment building of our friends on the West Side. The meter says $12.40. I pull a ten and a five from my wallet and lean forward to hand the money over the back of the seat.

"No, no," our driver says. "No charge. You are my guest."

"But I must pay something. This is your business."

"No. I cannot take your money. You have been my guest."

Pocketing my bills, my wife and I step from the cab. I turn, and in one of the few words of Urdu I remember from that trip so many years ago, I say, "*Meribani*." Thank you.

"*Shukriya*," he smiles back to me, and pulls away from the curb.

Muskrats

As I drove through a dense winter fog north on California's Route 101 to search out an old friend, sunshine and muskrats were on my mind. Back in July of 1956, between delivering the Daily Argus in Yonkers, New York, and playing games of stick ball and ring-a-levio on an asphalt parking lot wedged between red brick apartment buildings, I had a brief career as a fur trapper. My partner in that enterprise—let's call him Ben—was a twelve-year-old Huck Finn who had decided one bright summer afternoon that we could make our fortune by capturing muskrats out of the Bronx River and selling their pelts to John Wanamaker's fur department to be made into elegant stoles. Now, almost fifty years later, I'd tracked Ben down to a trailer parked under a stand of redwoods outside of the town of Occidental.

I'd called ahead, and after a bit of cajoling, he'd agreed to meet me for a beer. I'd only seen him a few times since he'd headed off to college in Montana. After many years of city living, he told me he longed for a green place where the air was clean.

He'd been drafted in 1966 and was sent to Vietnam a year later. I saw him when he got back, and over dinner at an Irish place on Third Avenue in New York, he told me about the Recon patrols that would make you shit your pants, the tracers at night that set fire to the sky while Jimi Hendrix blasted the night from someone's boom box, the dope and the whores that dulled the pain, and the dead kids. Lots of dead kids. I looked hard for the light in his eyes and the snap to his grin when he'd say, "Chuck you Farley and your whole Famdamnily," when anything got in his way. Instead, there was an emptiness.

Ben was two years older than I, and back in the summer of 1956, he was my best friend, better even than a big brother. In those days of rope swinging, stone skipping, and fort building, he seemed like freedom. There wasn't a tree he wouldn't climb, a culvert he wouldn't enter, a chain link fence he wouldn't scale. And I, holding my breath and gritting my teeth, would follow along pell mell.

He was the air itself, light and quick, though years later I would realize he'd been carrying extra weight. He lived with his mother in a walk-up apartment on the roof that was only a figurative step up from the super's dank basement room. Every morning, his mother would take the train into New York to work in a fragrance store down on 14th Street. She'd get home late or sometimes not at all. She slept on a fold-out couch in their small living room so that Ben could have the tiny bedroom. A kitchen with chipped appliances and a bathroom with a dripping shower made up the rest of their home. When she had company, Ben would spend the night at my place.

He seemed immune to the weather, venturing out in the rain in his torn sneakers. In the midst of winter, he'd run up to the school bus in a striped tee shirt with no jacket. "Cold doesn't bother me," he'd say, laughing into the wind. I'd unbutton my jacket to show him that I could take it, too but then gather my coat around me when he turned away. It wasn't until years later that it dawned on me he might not have had a jacket or boots to wear.

And he was tough. I once saw him go out for a long pass on the field nestled below the embankment to the Bronx River Parkway. The pie-shaped field had several ditches, many boulders, and a few, tall oak trees sprinkled about. It served as our baseball diamond, football field, war zone, and OK Corral. Running full out ahead of the ball, he looked over his shoulder and snagged it cleanly out of the air, turning his head to smash right into an oak tree. His nose spread out across his face, blood spurting down the front of his shirt. He moaned but didn't cry. I never saw him cry—not when he broke his arm, not when his father abandoned him, not even years later when he told me his mother killed herself by jumping off the roof of their apartment building down into the courtyard where we once played marbles. Me, I cried when King Kong got shot down from the top of the Empire State Building.

After Vietnam, he'd taken his army savings and bought five acres of redwoods in Northern California. Then he packed a duffle bag and booked passage on a freighter to the Far East. He wasn't a great letter writer though I did receive one from Indonesia and another from Borneo. They rambled on about strange foods and smells and people. And mushrooms. It was several years until I heard from him again.

But back in the summer of 1956, the sky was clear, and the summer was spread out before us. There was adventure in the air and muskrats in the river. Someone, Rick Ellrodt, I think, told us that he had heard from a friend who knew a guy who said that Wanamaker's was paying two-fifty for every muskrat skin to be made into elegant fur coats and stoles. At that time, my weekly allowance was fifty cents, and for that I had to take out the garbage. Two-fifty a pelt was a princely sum indeed.

Pooling our savings, Ben and I walked to Angelo's Sporting Goods over on Mount Vernon Avenue. The selection of traps was minimal. They had box traps that you baited inside with a door that slammed down to catch an animal alive. They cost three ninety-nine, or you could get steel traps with jaws that snapped shut on the critter's leg. They cost one twenty-five. Steel traps it was. At a buck and a quarter, we could afford three traps and figured we'd make back our investment and more with just two skins. Then it would all be profit.

The Bronx River at that time was nothing much more than an open sewer. Sometimes you could see the turds floating by. Our parents warned us that getting wet would mean a trip to the doctor for a tetanus shot or worse, so no one went swimming, but everyone got pushed in sooner or later. How bad could it be? After all there were muskrats.

We took our traps down to the river and spiked them into the ground at the water's edge near to the sewer pipes where we had seen most of the muskrats moving about. We pried open the steel jaws and set them on the ground, covering them with weeds and twigs. We placed a slice of Wonder bread near each trap. The hunt was on. We snuck back up the bank to hide among the brambles to wait for our prey. Of course, nothing happened, and after half an hour of slapping at mosquitos, we were hot and sweaty and bored with keeping quiet, so we decided to leave the traps overnight and return the next morning to collect our trophies.

At daybreak, we met under the Cross County Parkway Bridge. The cars and trucks hummed overhead, and their sweet, acrid exhausts drifted down to us. We made our way along the New York Central's right-of-way, walking on the rail ties and listening up for commuter trains. A year earlier, a kid from Tuckahoe had gotten creamed one afternoon on his way home from school. At the switching station, we clambered down the embankment to the shortcut to the river. At this early hour, the air was still crisp and the sky a bright blue. Our sneakers were soon soaked with dew. Before us, the brown river oozed, a few ducks circling around in the muck.

The first trap was undisturbed. The second was gone. Simply vanished. At the third, we hit pay dirt. There, caught in the jaws of the trap was a huge, hairy muskrat, very much alive. It shrank back from us, hissing and baring its teeth. Its right rear leg was a bloody mess where it had been snared in the steel jaws. My stomach flipped as I looked at this grisly scene, but Ben leaned over, picked up a rock and dropped it on the muskrat's head. At first stunned, the muskrat was dead after the fourth blow.

"What?" Ben asked.

"Nothing."

"You ain't gonna pussy out on me?"

"Nope."

"Okay, then, get the other trap."

I went back and took a stick and sprung the empty trap. I pulled up the stake and swung the trap over my shoulder. Ben pulled up the one with the muskrat and with the animal dangling from the jaws, carried it up the hill. At the top, he laid the muskrat down, and we stared at it.

"What now?" I asked.

"I guess we skin it," he said, pulling his black handled jackknife out of his pocket.

"You know what you're doing?"

"How hard can it be? You just cut the skin off."

So that's what he did. Somehow, I managed to keep my breakfast down and even helped to hold the carcass steady a few times as Ben hacked away. When the skin was off, all we could do was stare. Was someone really going to pay two dollars and fifty cents for this bloody mess? Only one way to find out.

Now, as I entered the small town of Occidental under a heavy cloud cover, I wondered what Ben would look like. I hadn't seen him for over twenty years. The last time had been in

Washington, DC, when he'd popped up on his way back to California. He'd been living out of his car for over a year, getting by on hand outs and crashing at shelters. I talked him into spending a night at my house, and after my wife went to bed, we stayed up drinking scotch and playing 'remember when.' He told me he had a Korean wife back in California who waited tables. He left the next morning in a snow storm.

I heard from Billy Koehler that Ben had ended up homeless on the streets of San Francisco for a few years but then moved up north, getting together again with his wife.

The last time we'd spoken was about ten years ago when he tracked me down in Virginia. I don't remember too much of the conversation. He had misjudged the time difference from the West Coast, awakening me from a deep sleep at three in the morning with his call. We promised to stay in touch but then didn't.

The lot next to the rundown bar and grill in Occidental was empty except for a few rusted trucks and one VW bus that looked like it had been parked there since the mid-sixties. The rain held off, but there was a mist in the air that fogged my glasses as I made my way to the door. I stepped into the gloom, wiping my lenses with a tissue and taking a moment for my eyes to adjust. There was a long, stained, mahogany bar with a cracked mirror along the wall reflecting the dusty inventory of bottles. There were a few tables and some booths in the rear, and I saw a cigarette glow in the farthest one at the back.

In 1956, Wanamaker's Department Store was over the highway in the Cross County Shopping Center, about a mile away from the Bronx River. The day had heated up by the time Ben and I got there. A salesman looked up from his shiny wooden desk as we entered the fur department. He wasn't smiling. Not too many kids came to his quiet area of the store, especially without any grown-ups in sight. The green carpet was plush and the coats, lining the walls, were trimmed in rich, lustrous furs. Having come straight from the river, we still had traces of mud on our sneakers and slime on our jeans. It wasn't surprising when the salesman bolted out of his chair before we could get close to any of his coats or stoles.

"What do you boys want?" he asked, wrinkling up his nose.

"We've got a fur to sell," said Ben.

"What?" He straightened his maroon silk tie.

"A fur. We heard you were paying two and a half bucks for muskrat furs." And with that, Ben opened the soggy paper bag and showed the man our trophy.

Wide-eyed, he jumped back a good three feet, screaming, "Get that goddamn thing out of here."

"But, mister–"

"You idiots. That's a goddamn river rat. There aren't any muskrats around here, and I don't buy them anyway. Get the hell out of here before I call the cops. A damn rat. Are you kids crazy? Probably got rabies."

On the walk back home, we ditched the rat skin in a trash barrel. We were poorer but I guess a little wiser about the world of commerce. All was not lost, though. We discovered that opening the traps and swinging them against each other's butts made a hell of a game. As long as you didn't hit bare skin, it just left a bruise but no blood. Soon, most of the kids in the neighborhood had traps, and we'd play complex games of war down in the field, yelling and snapping the traps in the warm, summer night air. That went on for about two weeks until Frankie Augustine broke his finger in one, and our parents confiscated all the traps. But by that time, we'd sort of moved on to dropping water balloons off the apartment rooftops, anyway.

Reaching the rear booth, I sat down opposite Ben and signaled the waitress for a couple of beers. Ben's face was pitted and lined, his beard shaggy and shot full of grey, and his eyes red-rimmed and glazed. We sat mostly in silence. I asked him, "How are you doing?"

"Not bad." He reached for another Camel and struck a match and raised the flame to the end of his cigarette. He blew smoke to the ceiling and, when his eyes lowered, he looked at me, squinting as if trying to recall who I was through the dim light.

I did most of the talking, reminiscing about the time we got arrested for the B-B gun, though they didn't actually arrest kids in those days. But we did get a ride in a police car. Then there was the incident with the cherry bomb, lighting up the whole field seconds after we ran smack into the two cops. And, oh yeah, there was that time we decided to kidnap Arnie Fox, the little shit. And remember when Frankie started up the bulldozer and drove it through that construction shed? I got a few nods, but mostly Ben just smoked and sipped at his beer and frowned across the room.

Then I asked, "Remember those muskrats?"

For a moment, as he looked up at me, those cloudy eyes cleared, and a smirk flashed at the edge of his mouth. But only for a moment.

Sisters

At the quiet hour between lunch and high tea, Julia Samuels had the hotel lounge to herself, except for the Sikh family across the room—a father, a mother, and two young sisters huddled together on an emerald green couch, sharing a confidence. The sisters giggled, and Julia smiled, though the girls, lost in their own world, didn't notice. Being an only child, Julia often wondered what it would have been like to have grown up bonded so closely to another. As Julia waited, a waiter crossed the ornate room with its ivory, silk brocade wallpaper, buffed marble floor with the scattering of worn oriental rugs, sparkling crystal chandeliers, and white stucco columns supporting arches intricately carved with elephants, tigers, and water buffalo. Dressed in a crisp white tunic and crimson turban, he approached and asked, "Would Madam care for another Nimbu Pani?"

"Yes, I believe I would. Thank you." She had come to favor this Indian lemonade with its freshly squeezed lemons and generous helping of sugar.

Julia had taken advantage of a lull in her schedule to book the guided tour to India. As they travelled through Rajasthan, their guide steered them to guesthouses and restaurants where the food was not too spicy, the water safe, and Westerners welcome. Even so, a number of their party had come down with Delhi-Belly, confined to their rooms for a day or two until antibiotics could counter their distress. Julia was proud she had not been sick. While others on the tour had pushed their curries and dals around their plates sipping on their bottled water, Julia had eaten adventurously, eating, as one member of their party had joked, as if trying to devour the sub-continent. The tour was now over— thanks given, baksheesh distributed, and flights caught, but she had remained behind for an additional five days in New Delhi.

"Thank you," she said, as the waiter placed a beaded glass before her. Taking a sip of her cool drink, she looked up to see an Indian woman dressed in a light blue sari, enter the lounge. The woman stood erect, taller than most Indian women. Her hair, streaked with gray, was pulled back and tied in a bun. Her skin was fair, as if she scrupulously avoided the sun, and her face smooth, except for the tiny laugh lines at the edges of her almond eyes. Those eyes, having searched the room, now rested on Julia. She approached, and Julia set down her glass and stood.

"Julia Samuels?"

"Anusha Sharma?"

"Yes, but please call me Anu. All my friends call me that."

As Julia stuck out her hand, Anu placed hers together in the Indian 'Namaste' greeting. Julia corrected herself, pressing her hands together just as Anu separated hers and reached for Julia's.

"Ha," Anu said. "East meets west. Why don't we just share a little hug?"

Julia stepped forward, tentatively placing her hands on Anu's shoulders, and softly kissed her cheek. The warmth of the day was still captured in the folds of the sari along with a scent of sandalwood. Anu wrapped her arms around Julia, pulling her close. Julia surprised herself when the first tear slid down her face.

"Sister," she whispered.

The secret had come out a year earlier, just after Julia's fifty-third birthday. She was packing up her father's Baltimore apartment as he prepared for the transition from home care to hospice. There was a cracked and taped manila folder labeled Anusha, containing a black and white photograph of a young girl dressed in a school uniform, standing with her arms crossed over her chest, her gaze looking off to the left avoiding the eye of the camera. There was a record of years of hundred-dollar checks and a bundle of aerograms, their sheer blue paper folded twice to make a lightweight letter, the stamps Indian.

"What's this, Dad?"

"Ah, Anusha. Yes, it's time to talk about her."

Soon after graduating from college, her father had secured a one-year internship with the Agency for International Development to work on a hydro-electric project in Northern India. He boarded with an Indian family, a doctor, his wife, and two children. The doctor's daughter was nineteen and a student at Delhi University. The son, a year younger, was in his last year at St. Stephens. When Julia's father's job ended, he returned to the States to pursue a PhD in civil engineering.

Three years after his return to Baltimore, he received a letter from the Indian doctor's wife. The doctor had suffered a stroke and could no longer work. There were money problems. They hadn't planned on contacting him but now had no choice. Their daughter had given birth to a child after his departure. They named the baby Anusha. And so began the payments, which went on for many years until he received a final letter from Anusha herself informing him she had completed her medical training and would no longer need or accept more money.

"Dad? You mean I have a sister, or half-sister?" Julia sat down on the couch clutching the folder to her chest. "But why keep this secret all these years? Did Mom know?"

"When I met your mother in graduate school, I didn't know. By the time Anusha's family contacted me, your mom and I were married. I didn't know how to raise the subject. As time went on, the secret grew. Then you were born, making it more complicated. After your mother died, I thought of mentioning it to you, but by then, the payments had ended, and it all seemed ancient history."

"And you never saw her? You never returned to India?"

"No. Of course, I was curious, but, except for the money, I was never encouraged to have any relationship with Anusha."

"And now?" Julia asked, sliding over on the couch to take her father's hand.

"If I didn't tell you now, there wouldn't be another chance. I should have told you earlier, your mother, too. And I should have reached out to Anusha, perhaps gone back to India." Her father, his shoulders slumped, looked past her with unfocused, watery eyes, as if trying to see another history. He took a breath and turned to Julia once again. "I want to leave Anusha something. I did some checking and found out she's a doctor running a clinic for the poor in Delhi. I'd like to bequeath a gift to the clinic on my death. When I die, you'll need to be the one to see she gets it."

The waiter crossed the lounge and set down an ice-filled glass and a bottle of Campa Cola before Anu. She took a sip and nodded her thanks. She turned to Julia and said, "I see a strong resemblance to your father, especially in your eyes."

"I didn't think you'd ever met my father."

"No, I did not, but my mother had a photo of him from his year with our family. She showed it to me when she explained his importance in our life. I remember how tenderly she held it. I think perhaps he was her one great love."

113

In the silence that followed, Julia searched Anu's face, looking for a flicker of her father—maybe something about the mouth and the set of the jaw and the smile. Yes, maybe the smile.

Anu leaned forward and broke the silence. "So, tell me about yourself."

"I'm a nurse working in a big hospital in Baltimore. I've just been named the head of my department, so before I start the new job, I grabbed this chance to come to India."

"A nurse. And the head of your department, too. Congratulations. So we're both in the medical field. Are you married?"

"No. Oh, there were men, but nothing stuck. I guess I'm married to my job."

"Just like me. Though in India, the whole marriage thing is so complicated. When the family discovered the truth about my mother, it became quite the scandal. There had to be a hurry-up wedding, but who would marry her? My grandfather found some wastrel and offered him a large dowry. After a couple of years, he absconded with the money and vanished. I think the whole thing soured me on marriage."

"And your mother?"

"Oh, she died many years ago. My mother had a younger brother, my uncle, but he is gone, too, so now I'm on my own."

"Like me."

"Yes, like you, married to our jobs. Speaking of which, would you like to see the clinic?"

They shared an auto-rickshaw, leaving behind the broad, shaded avenues of New Delhi for the old city's narrow, crowded alleyways with their blazing colors—saffron, ocher, indigo, crimson, and gold. Hawkers cried out selling fabrics, tin ware, rugs, jewelry, dal wrapped in freshly baked roti, yogurt lassis served out of earthenware cups, and betel nut wrapped in pan leaves. Motorcycles thundered by, and emaciated horses with their protruding ribs and boney hips limped along, pulling rattling tonga carts. Taxis and rickshaws sounded their horns, dodging cows and donkeys. Julia shut her eyes and inhaled the odors— roasting tandoori chicken, smoke from dung fires, cardamom, cumin, and coriander from the spice shops, and the thick foul emissions from the hundreds of lorries, buses, and cars.

Opening her eyes, Julia smiled and took Anu's hand, marveling at how now there was something where for so long there had been nothing.

Near Kashmiri Gate, they entered a quieter street and stopped in front of a three-story, grimy, tan stucco havali. A faded green balcony, rotting and hanging askew, fronted the second story, providing a perilous cover for the front door. At the curb before the building, a pig rooted in the trash. After paying off their driver, Anu shooed the pig, which snorted and meandered down the gutter.

Everything changed when they entered the building. The walls were whitewashed, the old marble floors scrubbed, and the sparse furniture polished. A nurse in a freshly starched white cotton sari trimmed in blue, rushed toward them, wringing her hands.

"Quick, Maa. There's been an accident."

Julia followed in Anu's wake as she rushed into the clinic's examination room. A dozen people had been hurt when a bus collided with a bullock cart not far from the clinic.

"This one to hospital, call them immediately. This one, too. The boy only needs a few stitches; the girl needs a compression bandage and a tetanus shot."

"Can I help?" Julia asked.

"Yes, please," Anu said. "Sister Lakshmi, help Sister Julia find a smock and gloves."

"Yes, Maa. Please Sister Julia, come with me."

Sisters. Here, in the British fashion, Julia realized, all the nurses were referred to as 'Sister.'

After hours of working side-by-side tending to the wounded, they had changed out of their smocks and gloves and showered off the blood and sweat. In Anu's modest flat in a quarter on the cusp between the old and new city, they shared a vegetable curry. Over a pot of chai, Julia put her feet up on an ottoman and said, "I'm exhausted but exhilarated, too. The way everyone worked so well together. Back in Baltimore, it's all rules and procedures and forms to fill out. Everyone watching the clock, counting the minutes until they can punch out, but working with the sisters today, it was like one big family all supporting each other."

"But you must be excited about your new responsibilities in Baltimore."

"Of course, it's a great honor, but it will mean more administrative duties, less actual nursing."

"And you'll miss that?"

"Yes, but it's a good job, pays a lot more, and the hours are more stable. Enough about me." Smiling, Julia placed her feet on the floor, reached into her purse, and retrieved an envelope which she slid across the table to Anu.

"And what is this?" Anu read the letter, then read it again more slowly. She held up the check then slipped them both back into the envelope, placing the package on the table between them. "I can't accept this."

"Of course you can," said Julia, taking a sip of her tea. "It's what our father wanted. It's what I want. After father died, I had no one. Now, I've found you, a sister, a family—"

"Julia—"

"Anu, this is what—"

"Julia, listen. I'm not your sister. Your father is not my father."

Julia set down her cup. "What? What do you mean?"

So Anu explained. Yes, Julia's father had an affair with the young Indian girl who would become Anu's mother. After Julia's father left India, the younger brother, in a heated moment, told the family. After a hurry-up wedding, the husband soon disappeared with the dowry and other monies, leaving behind a baby, Anu.

"But your fair complexion?" Julia asked.

"My family is from the north, Kashmiris, descendants of the army of Alexander the Great some contend. We all have fair skin."

"But the letters, the requests for money?" Julia asked, folding her hands in her lap, trying to quell their trembling.

"Ah, yes, not one of our proudest moments. After my grandfather's stroke, the family was desperate. My grandmother came up with the idea of contacting your father. She knew he had a good heart, and in part because of his affair with my mother, she held him partly responsible for the aftermath and their dire condition. Anyway, they thought all Americans were rich. Of course, I was just a baby and knew nothing of this until years later. Just before she died, my mother told me the whole story. I wrote to your father informing him of my mother's death and of my graduation from medical school and asked him to halt the payments."

"Why didn't you tell me this earlier? Why let me go on believing and making a fool of myself?"

"I don't think you're foolish. I'm the fool. I'm alone, too. I enjoyed the idea of a sister. I didn't think it would hurt for the few days you were here. I knew you would return to the U.S., and it was unlikely we would ever see each other again. I thought I could just enjoy a few days of make-believe. I'm sorry."

"Then, why tell me?"

Anu reached down and tapped the envelope. "The money. It's gone too far. It would be stealing."

"Oh, the money. Forget the money. The money doesn't matter. Anyway, it's not for you; it's for the clinic. Take it. Buy Band-Aids or something."

"Band-Aids? Is that what you think we do here, Julia? Is that what you think of us?"

"No, of course not. It's just…I don't know what to think. For fifty years, I was an only child. Then my father was dying, and I thought I would be alone. Then, I learned I had a sister. Now, I learn I don't."

"I'm sorry this is so distressful for you."

"And not for you?"

"Of course, for me, too. I've had the same longing for family, for a sister, but I always knew the truth."

"I need to get back to my hotel. Can you call me a cab?"

"Julia, don't be upset. Don't rush off to your hotel. I saw you today. You're a wonderful nurse. You have skills we know nothing about here, but more importantly, you have a gentle, caring manner. Sister Lakshmi commented on it, how you dealt with each patient as a person, as someone to be valued, sharing compassion as well as medicine. Stay with us, with me, for the few days you have left before you return to Baltimore."

"No, I'm too confused. I need to be alone for a while."

For the remainder of the week, Julia stayed close to the hotel, sitting by the pool, taking her meals in the dining room or calling room service. She ventured out a couple of times to buy the few gifts she needed for her colleagues back in Baltimore: a red silk scarf, a pair of silver earrings, and some colored bangles. Several times she reached for the phone to call Anu, but her disappointment, her hurt, the betrayal stayed her hand. In the evenings, she retreated to the hotel's rooftop pub and looked out over the city, sparkling with thousands of lights. In the distance, fireworks exploded in the night sky. Diwali was beginning, the waiter told her, the festival of lights with fireworks and gifts and the promise of renewal.

A part of her was anxious to get back to Baltimore and to her new job, to her small but well-organized apartment, to the familiar streets, shops, and restaurants that made up her real life; a part of her despaired—to what was she really returning? A life with no family, no real friends? If she was honest with herself, she was returning to a sterile world, now to be made up of even safer and more comfortable routines and denied the hands-on nursing she loved. Yet she couldn't see any way to change direction, certainly not at this late stage. So, on her last evening in New Delhi, she found herself at the airport with her return ticket in hand.

"So sorry, Madam, flight has been cancelled. Mechanical problem. No flights possible until tomorrow night at the earliest."

"But what am I to do?"

"I suggest you return to your hotel."

"But I've checked out. I heard them say they were fully booked for the next few days."

"Ah, yes, Diwali. I'm afraid all hotels will be booked. Have you no other place to stay?"

Julia directed the taxi to the three-story stucco havali not far from the Kashmiri Gate. The flickering lights from the dozens of tiny oil lamps lining the sagging balcony illuminated the front of the building. She entered the quiet reception room, and a sleepy-eyed Lakshmi raised her resting head and smiled.

"Maa," she called out over her shoulder, "Come see. Sister Julia's here."

Summer Begins

My father reaches around from behind his Wall Street Journal to hook his finger through the handle of his stained coffee cup. The cup disappears behind the wall of print. It is the first day of my summer vacation, but summer has yet to begin. With a click, the minute hand of the kitchen clock jumps forward to rest on the six. My father lowers his paper, looks up, and says, "Right."

He rises, folding the paper and setting it down next to his cup and the yolk-smeared plate strewn with the gnawed crusts from his toast. He picks up the grey suit jacket from the back of his chair and without another word leaves for his job teaching at summer school.

The screen door slams. My mother sits up taller and exhales, her eyes wandering over to the red dress draped over the banister leading upstairs. My sister jumps up and twirls across the hardwood floor in a series of frenzied pirouettes.

Outside bicycle bells ring, a basketball thumps against a nearby driveway, and morning sprinklers swish fans of cool water. The scent of newly cut grass fills my head.

"Let the summer begin," I say.

And it does.

The Lady in the Window

After two weeks of living out of a suitcase in the Drake Hotel a couple of blocks from Central Park, the rental agent called once more to tell me that she had found a furnished sublet over on Third Avenue at 23rd Street. The owners were off on an extended cruise through the Far East, and I could have the place through February. Having seen one too many over-priced dumps during the past two weeks, my expectations weren't high as I entered the elevator and rose to the 28th floor, yet now I stood in the very lap of luxury. The apartment had everything I could possibly want: a living room with an adjoining dining area, a bedroom with a spacious bed and lots of closet space, a study with high-speed Internet access, and even a recently remodeled gourmet kitchen with granite counter tops and stainless-steel appliances.

Over the steam rising from a cup of freshly brewed coffee, I surveyed the New York skyline, scanning eastward from the Empire State Building to the Chrysler Building to the East River, which sparkled below on this crystalline autumn day. I thought, 'It doesn't get any better than this,' when it did. There across 23rd Street in an apartment window a couple of floors below mine stood a naked woman doing some sort of aerobic workout. An omen I was sure, and I signed the necessary papers for the lease on the spot.

"That should do it, Mr. Hightower."

"Please, Pamela, call me Nigel." Though my hair was shot with grey and I wouldn't be running any marathons in the near future—not that I ever did, I found it a bit off-putting to be referred to so formally by a woman well over thirty. I wasn't that old.

"Of course. Well, Nigel, if there is anything else I can do for you during your stay in the city, just let me know," she said, extending her hand.

"Thank you. I suspect everything is going to be just fine," and with a firm shake of her hand, she was gone. I locked the door behind her and scurried over to the window, but alas, my nudist exerciser had vanished. Still it was a beautiful day, and my spirits were high.

I had come to New York at the behest of Stanley Granger, the CEO of Paragon Books, for a three-month spell to edit Walter Emerson's new novel. Usually, Stanley let me conduct my editorial duties from my home office in the Uptown neighborhood of New Orleans. Having been with Paragon since Stanley took over the company more than twenty years ago in 1988 and having shepherded in more than my share of bestsellers over the years, Stanley gave me a great deal of leeway in my affairs. So, when Veronica, my wife of twenty-five years, received an attractive offer from a major law firm in New Orleans, Stanley agreed to my relocating to the Crescent City provided my work didn't suffer. It didn't, and most of my writers seem to enjoy working with me in New Orleans and skipping the New York rat race, with the notable exception of Walter.

I suspect you remember Walter Emerson. In the early Nineties, he had two back-to-back bestsellers: The Nighthawks, the title borrowed from Edward Hopper's painting of the same name, and Granger's Lane, the title being a sort of insiders' homage to Stanley who was the first to recognize Walter's genius and to publish him. Both books were part of my early editorial successes, and both spent several months near the top of the New York Times' best sellers list. What readers remember most about the books are the vivid descriptions of the New York club scene. The main characters where *Innocents*, pulled down into the depths of depravity and then asked to crawl back out in acts of personal redemption. The books had it all: sex, drugs, and rock and roll, and the loss of soul and ultimate deliverance through love. Jesus, how they sold. Stanley had pulled off the publishing coup of the decade, I was sought out as an editor by established writers interested in supercharging their careers, and Walter…. Well, Walter was hailed as the next Hemingway (or Fitzgerald or Salinger depending on who was writing the review), the savior of the novel, and the best of his generation. He was on the cover of *Time* and profiled in *Esquire*, *Playboy*, and *Vanity Fair*… the toast of the town. The king of the hill. Then…. Well, then there was silence. The third book never came. Oh, he teased us over the years with a short story here and an essay there, but as for another masterpiece—nothing.

Some said that Walter had done a tad too much research into the underbelly of the city and had become addicted to cocaine, alcohol, kinky sex—take your pick. Others thought some kind of cult was involved with his disappearance from the literary scene after he wrote that piece on UFOs for *The New Yorker*. The truth was, of course, far more mundane. His two books had made Walter a very rich man. He had a brownstone in the Village and a weekend retreat on Shelter Island. He had a Mercedes town car and a restored red '58 Triumph TR3 in which he bombed around the island. In the past twenty years, he'd married and divorced three lovely ladies and had half a dozen children who adored him.

He was now working on the fourth wife—a younger, more fashionable, richer version of the others, a woman pursuing her PHD at Columbia in American Letters—another perfect match. He had numerous literary and artistic friends, and he could always count on a good table at even the trendiest restaurant. And he was happy, content. And he stopped writing.

There's a fellow called Maslow, a sociologist. He developed something called the hierarchy of needs. Supposedly, each of us is motivated to work, to succeed, by certain needs. The most primitive driver is for food and shelter, like those poor souls you see on TV in India or Mexico or wherever who will do just about anything for a Rupee or a Peso or whatever. Higher up on the ladder are those seeking security or recognition. At the top of the hierarchy are the *self-actualizers*. This is where we find the writers, the artists, the thinkers. Having taken care of more basic needs, either through self-denial or the acquisition of wealth (or at least pulling together enough to get by on) one is supposedly free to realize the person one was meant to be. Thus, we imagine great artists do what they do because they want to or have to. They are living out their dreams. And I guess most of them are doing just that.

But every now and then, someone of great talent comes along like Walter who gets stuck on a lower rung of the ladder and who simply does what he does for the money. Marlon Brando seemed to be of this type. After *A Streetcar Named Desire* and *On the Waterfront*, he was hailed as an acting genius with the most promising of careers, but he seemed to act only enough to replenish his bank account so that he could traipse off to Tahiti and eat his way through the next fifty years. Oh, he'd pop up every now and then and dazzle us once again as the Godfather or Kurtz in *Apocalypse Now*, but then he'd cash his paycheck and abandon us for the luau. Bobby Fisher and Mike Tyson strike me as fellows cut from the same cloth.

So, when Stanley called me last October and told me Walter was writing again, my first words were, "Don't give him any more of an advance." There was silence on the other end, and I knew my warning had come too late. It took a good year for Walter to blow through that money, and now he appeared to be seriously at work. I'd seen a couple of chapters in the past few weeks though Walter was usually loath to part with anything until the manuscript was complete. However, he'd lost most of his bargaining chips, and Stanley had flat out refused a further advance until something was put on the table. The chapters were good but barely so. It would be hard for someone of Walter's recognized talent to write poorly; in fact, some of the passages were as good as he had ever produced, but it was all character and scene. It didn't seem to go anywhere. It was entirely derivative of his earlier work... nothing new. It was as if he had just added on a couple of unneeded sections to one of his earlier books. It was going to take a lot of late nights to pull together anything remotely publishable, much less a blockbuster to say nothing of an important literary work.

On the evening of the day I signed the lease on the apartment, I met Walter over at Elaine's on East 86th Street. The restaurant had maintained its cachet and was still the haunt of writers and artists, but like most of its clientele, the place had seen better days. It was living off a reputation from another era, as were many of its diners. New York had banned smoking in restaurants several years ago, but the place still seemed stuffy and stale.

Of course, I'd seen Walter in the intervening twenty years since his last novel, but we hadn't met since the year before I had relocated to New Orleans. The past four years hadn't been kind to him. He'd put on several pounds, and he had not been a lean man to start with. Short of stature, he was unfortunately beginning to resemble Mickey Rooney in his later years. His hair had always been thinning, and now he had taken the drastic step of shaving his head à la Bruce Willis or Michael Jordan. While a bald pate appeared youthful, vigorous, and devil-may-care on those gentlemen, on Walter it looked almost cartoonish—sort of like Elmer Fudd. His pasty complexion and the several large liver spots on his head didn't help matters.

I pulled out one of the wobbly wooden chairs and joined Walter at a table in the rear. We decided on martinis, not because either of us drank them anymore, but they had been what we drank back in the early nineties when we first worked together and our stars were rising in concert. Walter kindly asked after Veronica and our new life in New Orleans. I inquired about Millicent, the new wife, remembering her name in just the nick of time. We bantered back and forth a while like this, and then I asked him how the writing was going. He responded by ordering another martini. When we had our drinks, I pressed him a bit more.

"Seriously, Walter, Sidney tells me it's about done. Is it?"

"Well, something's about done. I've got about 500 pages, but I wouldn't say it was done. You saw a couple of chapters. What did you think?"

I fortified myself with a sip of my martini. "Interesting. Promising. I see potential in the main protagonist. He reminds me of you."

"Of course, he reminds you of me. It is me. It's always me. But 'promising,' 'interesting,' 'potential.' Is it really that bad?"

I hid my response in another belt of booze.

"Of course, it is," he continued. "I may be a washed-up writer, but I can still read." He put his head in his hands, pressing his pudgy fingers into his shiny skull. "Usually, when I find a character, he's strong enough to carry me along and the story just unfolds. This time though, I can't seem to get him going anywhere but in circles. I want the story to be about redemption. Don't look at me that way, Nigel, I know it's been done before. Christ, I've done it before. Twice in fact. But now I want to do it from the perspective of middle age."

"Middle age?"

"Fuck, Nigel, I'm only sixty-one. That's middle age these days."

Well, I could see we were in a bit of a tight place. Stanley was expecting a bestseller. I had just taken a three-month lease on a sublet to edit a masterpiece, and Walter was having writer's block. Well, not exactly writer's block; he had knocked out some 500 pages by his account, but was any of it any good? One had to have more than an interesting character and some elegant prose, one needed a story. We agreed to meet at my new apartment the next morning for breakfast when Walter would bring along what he'd written to date.

The next morning Walter was late but only by a half an hour. His eyes were red and his complexion more shallow than usual.

"Late night?" I asked.

"Yes, but not for the reasons you probably think. I actually read through all of this again. You know, some parts are quite good, and no one is a harsher critic of my work than me. Great character, some wonderful descriptions, spicy dialogue. It's just the plot. Why does the main character decide to reinvent himself, to save himself? What's the motivation? The orphan girl just isn't convincing."

Orphan girl? I asked myself. Had Walter written *Little Orphan Annie, Part II?*

I'd cleared the dining room table and now suggested Walter lay out the novel while I made a fresh pot of coffee. When I returned to the dining room with two steaming cups, I checked my watch and said, "Before we start, you've got to see this."

We walked over to the window and stood before the New York panorama. There was fog this morning over the East River, and the spires of the Brooklyn Bridge barely broke through the mist into the sunlight. "I love living in the Village," Walter said, taking a sip from his cup, "but you sure don't get views like this."

"Not the view, though I agree it is spectacular. Look at the building across the way, two stories down toward the middle."

And there she was in all her glory. The morning light pouring into her window served as nature's spotlight. Her skin was glistening from exertion. Her auburn hair hung free and bounced with the music only she could hear. It must have been something with a robust tempo judging from the unpredictable volatility of the other parts of her body. Walter stood transfixed, the cup raised half way to his gaping mouth.

"That's it," he said.

I laughed. "Well, yes, I guess that's one way of putting it. Now that you've had your morning coffee and voyeuristic fix, what do you say we get to work?"

"No, no. That's it. That's the vehicle for redemption. Don't you see it? At his moment of greatest despair, he looks out the window and sees a naked woman dancing in the sunlit window across the street. Now he must find out who she is. Will she save him? Won't she? Will he save himself through her? Or by saving her does he redeem himself? Does he lose himself in the process or find himself? Yes, I can see it. I can see it."

With that, Walter set down his coffee cup, gathered up his papers, and bolted from the apartment. By the time I returned to the window, the lady was gone.

I didn't see Walter for the rest of the winter. According to Sidney, he spent it hard at work. With the apartment leased for three months, I spent my time in New York working with other authors and trying to get back to New Orleans at least every other weekend. Veronica was consumed with major litigation involving an oil spill in the Gulf, so my absence wasn't too much of a strain on our marriage. During this whole period, I never saw the naked dancer again. Perhaps she had joined a nudist health club, if there are such things.

When Walter submitted his manuscript in the spring, I was back in New Orleans. Sidney wanted me to return to New York to edit the book, but after reading it through once, I knew that wouldn't be necessary. It was perfect. Oh, I had a few minor suggestions, but they were of little consequence. Walter had written the masterpiece we all had hoped for. I was touched when the book was published and I read the dedication: To Nigel Hightower who showed me the way. The Lady in the Window spent thirty-two weeks on the *New York Times* Best Sellers list and made both Sidney and Walter fortunes all over again.

Sidney tells me that Walter hasn't written a word since.

The Man with No Nose

A few months after moving to India in 1959, I passed a leper sitting on a ragged and dirty dhurrie on the side of the road. He shared the ratty carpet with his wife and baby daughter, all crowded together before a small, chipped bowl. The leper had stubs for fingers, open white sores on his bare legs above his rag-wrapped feet and a perpetual smile on his face caused by the absence of his upper lip. Where his nose should have been, there was only a hole. His wife looked thin and gaunt but showed no sign of the disease. As I approached, she gathered the end of her pale-yellow, cotton sari over her head and across her mouth. As her gurgling baby nestled in her arms, she surveyed me over the edge of her sari as her husband called out for alms. The baby squealed happily, and both parents leaned in to coo at it. Once again, I was puzzled at how, in the midst of this poverty and horror a moment of happiness, even joy, could arise.

We had arrived in Delhi four months earlier from New York. I was fourteen years old and had recently graduated from Lincoln Junior High School in Yonkers. I had said goodbye to my friends and accompanied my father to India where we would live while he made documentary films for the United Nations.

On the day of our arrival in Delhi, as the towering thunderheads of the north Indian monsoon parted to let the sun shine briefly on a slick, water-logged road, I saw a naked boy with a swollen, brown belly run after a glistening, ebony water buffalo. Clutching a wooden bowl in his pencil-thin arms, he chased the loping beast down a slippery, trash-strewn, open sewer bordering a shantytown constructed from mud, thatch, and odd bits of rusted, corrugated sheet metal. The child had spotted a certain twitch in the buffalo's tail, and, having outraced the rest of the pack of three-year olds, he triumphantly raised his container under the animal just has its tail rose and a jet stream of hot dung shot forth, most of it landing in the bowl. A small girl, naked except for the half dozen red and green bangles dangling on her tiny wrist, was second on the scene and scooped up the dollops of muck that had splattered to the ground. Struggling under the load, the boy smiled and somehow managed to stagger over to one of the mud huts where his mother greeted him with a hug and a laugh. The mother then squatted on her haunches, reached into the steaming pile and grabbed a handful of dung, forming a patty, which she slapped on the wall of their hut to dry in the sun before the rains resumed. Later she would use this as fuel for their evening's fire on which she would cook rice and lentils and warm flat chapattis.

I knew about poverty, or I thought I did. I'd taken the train into New York City on countless occasions, rumbling through Harlem and staring into the vacant faces gazing back at the train from tenement windows. I'd overheard a conversation about a friend of my parents losing his job and the concerns with making the payments on his new car. Edward R. Murrow ran T.V. reports on the poor in Appalachia and in the slums of Detroit, complete with film clips of children without shoes. I'd seen old, grainy footage of soup kitchens in the Depression, and men in threadbare coats waiting in long unemployment lines, and I'd watched "The Grapes of Wrath" with Henry Fonda. I knew kids at school who ate the same sandwich with one slice of bologna every day for lunch, always forgetting to bring their milk money, and who wore the same, ratty Keds to school day after day regardless of the weather. They were the kids who never could join us for the Saturday twenty-five cent matinee at the Parkway Theatre over in Mt. Vernon but who were always hanging around when the show was over.

Well, if I knew what poverty was, what was this before me? What do you call a three-year old naked boy with a swollen belly carrying a bowl full of excrement? And why was he smiling? And why was his mother laughing?

When I arrived in India in 1959, almost half the population lived in poverty. That meant over 200 million people were impoverished. Since then, India has made great strides in reducing the degree of poverty from 50 to 20 percent, yet now with its population of 1.2 billion, almost three times its size in 1959, more than 250 million Indians remain destitute.

Today, in the United States about 40 million people are considered to be living in poverty, but in the United States, one is considered poor if his or her income drops below $10,000 a year (or below $22,000 for a family of four.) In India, the poverty level is pegged at $365 per person or around a dollar a day. None of this is to imply that there aren't people in the U.S. suffering greatly, but by almost any measure of poverty: money, food, clean water, electricity, education, or healthcare, poverty in India is in a league of its own. So it was in 1959, and even with the remarkable gains made by India in the past half century, so it remains today.

During my first weeks in India, I saw lots of naked children playing in the mud. The more fortunate were clothed but not in any clothing I'd seen before. These were basically rags, hung together in the semblance of clothing. And there were beggars, lots of beggars, most of them children or mothers cradling glassy-eyed infants in their arms. When the begging children approached, I'd empty my pockets of annas and rupees, but the hands kept reaching out.

Yet often when I'd finally broken free of pleading cries and grasping hands, I'd turn back and see the once desperate children laughing, dancing, pushing at each other, or kicking a half-inflated football through a goal post improvised from two discarded bricks. In the midst of this dreadfulness, from where did this capacity for playfulness arise?

Soon after my days of handing out money, I was advised to stop.

"You're just throwing money down a bottomless well, wishing for a miracle that isn't going to happen," said an Indian colleague of my father's.

"If you really want to help," advised a British development official, "give your money to one of the aid organizations. That's how one makes a difference."

"You understand that the kids don't get to keep the money. The crime syndicates control all the begging. They even blind and maim the kids to make them more pathetic. You shouldn't encourage this," said an older classmate at my new school.

And so, I learned to keep my coins in my pocket and to gaze past the crying, pleading faces.

In the United States, we view poverty with dread and the poor as somehow flawed. Maybe not as a result of their own actions, but somehow flawed nevertheless. We even fear the poor. If a homeless man approaches us on the street, we'll avert our eyes, ignore him, and cross to the other side. We may feel pity, we may feel compassion, but if we're honest with ourselves, we'll also admit to feeling revulsion and fear. Perhaps this aversion will be tinged with humility, as in "There but for the grace of God go I." The fear may be more basic as in "He's probably crazy—or drunk or drugged or off his meds or violent, or just out of jail." Or maybe our reaction will be more derisive as in "Why doesn't he get a job?"

In India, it was different. The poor were more accepted and even had a certain nobility. I'm not suggesting that India as a country wasn't serious about trying to alleviate poverty and improve conditions for the poor. It was and still is, but as a society, Indians granted the poor a degree of respect and honor. Maybe this was part and parcel of the caste system and Karma—everyone having a God-given role to play in this life in preparation for the next. Though India ostensibly abolished the caste system in 1960, as it was alive and well in 1959, it remains so today. To over simplify a complex structure, one is born into one of four religious and societal roles: priest, warrior, merchant, or servant. Outside of this system are the Dalits or Untouchables—really nonpersons and often considered to be sub or nonhuman. Though this term was outlawed with Independence in 1949, it still persists. The Untouchables are the ones who take care of unclean, polluting activities, such as maintaining sewers, sweeping floors, discarding dead animals, and lowly manual labor. These unclean activities render them Untouchable. Gandhi recognized the nobility in these tasks and coined the term Harijan, Children of God, to describe the Dalits.

Though Dalits are outside the caste system and are referred to as Outcasts, they are not outcasts, as we would use the term. They may be outside the formal caste system, but their activities are central to society's functioning. One activity reserved for the Untouchables is the maintenance of the Ghats, the steps to the riverbank where Hindus traditionally cremate their dead. So though Untouchable and poor, everyone, Brahmins (priests) included, have to come to the Ghat workers eventually for their services. They are indispensable to the smooth functioning of society. As poor as they are, they are necessary, and through that necessity gain a degree of self-respect and pride.

And so, the poor were less victims to be feared or pitied and more accepted as having an essential, predetermined role to play in society. Maybe this acceptance is what let begging children return to their game of football and to dancing and singing after being handed a few coins. Maybe this is what allowed a small child with a swollen belly and bearing a bowl filled with dung to smile and saunter over to his grateful mother and allowed her, in turn, to laugh. Or maybe it was just a testament to the resilience of love and joy even in the bleakest of conditions.

Therefore, as the days progressed, my view of the poor changed. My fear and distaste receded and was replaced by a comfort and acceptance. I no longer looked away or failed to return a greeting, though as advised, I kept my annas and my rupees to myself, that is until I met the man with no nose.

My school was located in a residential neighborhood of New Delhi. After class and school activities, I'd hop a bus over to Connaught Place and then walk the four or five blocks to the U.N. office. I'd spend an hour in the Information Center's library doing homework before riding back with my father to our home in the old city. Along the way to my father's office, I passed the leper's family. Though I was no longer giving handouts to begging children, I dropped four annas into the leper's bowl, as the family huddled together on their worn rug, the parents fussing over their cooing baby. In those days, four annas equaled about a nickel, but that was at a time when many workers would feel lucky to make a rupee or twenty cents for a day's hard labor. Four annas would buy a meal of rice and vegetables for the three of them.

Dropping four annas into their bowl became my routine. We got to the point where instead of the leper waving his damaged hands in the air and crying out to me for alms, we would exchange 'Namastes', and I'd say something nice about the baby, which I'm sure neither he nor his wife could understand. One day, the wife smiled instead of covering her head with the end of her sari.

The winter holiday for our school arrived, a combination of Diwali and Christmas, and for almost two weeks, I didn't go to school and didn't see the leper and his family. When I appeared, they were agitated and to my eye looked more gaunt, if that was even possible. The man's tone was harsh. That day I left a whole rupee in their bowl. Soon, we had returned to our routine, and the smiles returned.

Then, one day they weren't there. Nor the next. Nor over the next two weeks. After that, I took another route to my father's office so that I wouldn't have to walk by the vacant curb, and, once again, I kept my annas to myself.

The Coat

T he mix-up occurred on a Tuesday evening on the 6:28 express from Grand Central to Bronxville. Mallory had suggested martinis at the Oyster Bar before catching our respective trains to celebrate the 1985 Architect Institute Award our firm had landed that day. Mallory was the managing partner at Tomlin and Sanford, and we did have reason to celebrate. I'd spent long, grueling hours of drudgery translating his design into the blueprints needed for our winning submission, a detail Tomlin himself remembered at the mid-afternoon announcement. I arrived at the bar a few minutes late, dusting the newly fallen snow from my overcoat and spotted Mallory sipping his drink.

"Can't fly home on one wing, Trevor," he said, after we'd downed our first martini.

With two quick drinks under my belt, I rushed to catch the 6:28, arriving just as the conductor yelled out "All aboard," and the grey metal doors slammed shut behind me. I stumbled through three jostling compartments before finding an empty seat next to a fellow leaning against the smudged window sound asleep. From the way in which he propped his head while tilting his legs toward the aisle, I could see he suffered from the same problem I endure. Chaps of our frame can't slip easily into airline, bus, or railway seats. I could have awakened him and asked he contort himself further to provide me with more room, but years of grappling with the same issue left me sympathetic. I edged in next to him and settled myself as best I could, placing my brown, scuffed briefcase between my feet and twisting my knees sideways into the aisle.

Winter had descended on Manhattan, and the carriage was soon overheated in preparation for the train's emergence from the tunnel into the frigid night air of Harlem just north of Central Park. Though I usually complete the Times' crossword puzzle on the ride home, on this evening, I couldn't muster the energy. My next conscious moment came with the conductor announcing my stop.

"Bronxville. Bronxville. Next stop Tuckahoe."

My head snapped up, and my eyes tried to focus in the bright, florescent lights of the railway car. Outside, I could see snow falling on the station's platform. I shook myself awake, stood, grabbed my briefcase from the floor, snatched my coat from the overhead rack, and stumbled to the doorway of the compartment.

The train began to move as I stepped on to the icy platform. I set down my briefcase, and as I tried to wrestle my arm into the sleeve of the coat, I realized I was already wearing mine. In my haste and sleepy confusion, I'd grabbed the other gentleman's garment. I looked down the tracks through the swirling snow at the receding red taillights of the train as it slipped into the dark night.

Once home, my wife, Pris, poured me another martini, which I decidedly didn't need but was part of our nightly routine, and we sat down to watch the last half of the seven o'clock news. While we watched *Jeopardy*, we had a light dinner. This being Thursday, it was chicken pot pie. At eight, I retreated to my study to put in my customary hour or so of work to prepare for the next day, but I was too distracted to accomplish anything, so I retrieved the coat from the hallway where I had left it.

It was a well-made, dark grey cashmere much like my own. There was no nametag or other identification. A search of the pockets wasn't much help either: a pair of fleece-lined, brown leather gloves; a half-full pack of Camels, unfiltered; some tissues, which I discarded; a matchbook, with Café Milan inscribed on the cover along with an address in Little Italy; and a betting slip from Yonkers Raceway. I took a small bit of comfort from the fact there were no keys or wallet in the coat. At least I hadn't left him locked out or destitute. The last item in his pocket was a bit troubling—a bullet.

I decided to place an ad in the Times, and each evening for the rest of the week, I got to the 6:28 early and stood by the gate visibly holding the coat and scanning the boarding passengers for someone of my build—all to no avail.

On Saturday afternoon, I begged off our usual trip to the grocery store and told Pris I had a few errands to run. Putting on the filched coat, I drove to Yonkers Raceway. The trotters weren't running at that hour, but the clubhouse was quite lively with the advent of Off Track Betting and the television hook-ups to racetracks all around the world.

The bar was doing a good business, and I sat down on a red vinyl stool and ordered a Heineken. The people milling about were older, many with grey hair and greyer complexions. I looked down at my hand and realized that I had extracted the half-full pack of Camels from the pocket of the coat. I hadn't had a cigarette since college and considered smoking to be a vile habit. I shook one out, and it slid between my fingers. I tamped one end on the bar and raised it to my lips. I struck a match, the flare of the igniting sulfur stinging my nostrils. The first drag wafted me back to dark cellars and loud music and gyrating, sweaty bodies and wet, lingering kisses, now belonging only to the past. The smoke made me a touch dizzy, too.

I stubbed out the cigarette and caught the barkeep's eye.

"Excuse me," I said. "I'm not quite sure what to do with this." I dug the betting slip out of my pocket.

"Is it a winning ticket?" he asked, wiping the counter with a ratty rag.

"Well, I don't know. You see I found it, sort of."

"Well, if you found it, sort of, it was probably tossed because it was a loser. If you want to make sure, take it over to one of those betting windows."

I strolled up to the first window and bent down so that I could see beyond the grate. A middle-aged woman, a bit on the heavy side, was looking down through pink-framed glasses reading a form. I cleared my throat, and she peered up.

"I wonder if you could check on this ticket for me," I said, sliding it through the opening.

She glanced at it. "This is dated last week. The 6th Anaheim race."

She punched some numbers into a machine and extracted some bills from her drawer and slid them toward me. I could see several hundreds and a few twenties.

"Is there any way you could tell who bought this ticket?"

"No, hon, but you still gotta report it to the IRS as income."

I walked from the window counting my winnings. Well, not mine, of course, but winnings nonetheless. Eight hundred and sixty-two dollars. I folded the bills into my trouser pocket.

As I drove away, I wondered why someone would walk around with a betting slip worth more than eight hundred dollars stuffed into his overcoat pocket. Why hadn't he cashed it on the day of the race? I was determined to solve the mystery and to locate the owner of the ticket and the coat.

On my way home, I swung by the library. I sat in front of the microfiche reader holding my next clue, in fact the only other one—the matchbook with the name Café Milan. I found a number of New York Post articles referencing the club dating back a year ago. There'd been some speculation the café was a money-laundering operation for the Cosa Nostra. The police had even arrested a Mafia capo as he exited the bar. I put my hand in my pocket and hefted the bullet I'd found in the coat. It was heavier than I remembered. I stepped out into the late afternoon cold, and as I peeled away another match to light a cigarette, I noticed a number scribbled on the inside of the matchbook cover. I tilted it toward the sun and saw a 212 area code—New York City. I rushed home to call it.

"Fantasy Escort Service."

I hung up the phone. An escort service. I'd never met an escort. Never talked with one. I knew many such services were cover operations for prostitutes. Had I just talked with a prostitute? I leaned back in my chair, and after peering through the door of my study to ensure that Pris wasn't nearby, I redialed.

"Hey, did you just call and hang up?" asked a woman with a sultry timbre to her voice.

"Me? Ah, no. No. I'm just calling.... You see I have your number on a matchbook. Café Milan. In Little Italy."

"Yeah. I remember you. Jack Daniels on the rocks. This is Melissa. Last Thursday. No I guess it was a week ago Thursday. So, you decided to call."

"Well, yeah. You see—"

"Look, I gotta run. I've a client waiting. You gonna be at Café Milan on Thursday again?"

"Thursday. Sure. I guess."

"Okay. Around five?"

"Maybe a bit later."

"Okay, see you at six."

Had I really just made a date with a prostitute in a Mafia run bar in Little Italy?

It was sleeting on Thursday evening, and I wore the purloined coat with the hope that the woman I was to meet would recognize it. The bar was dimly lit, and it took a moment for my eyes to adjust to the gloom. It was one of those places with dark wood and red leather chairs and votive candles flickering on each table. Groups, mostly men in dark suits and white shirts, murmured around the tables. Their eyes shifted toward me. A woman at the end of the bar waved. I made my way down a line of serious drinkers bent over their glasses and took the stool next to hers. She was in her early thirties, about ten years younger than me, and quite attractive in that obvious sort of way. I focused on her heavily mascaraed eyes, willing myself not to lower my gaze to her ample bosom.

"Hey, wait a minute, you're not Ted. Did he give you my number?"

"Sort of," I explained.

"So, this isn't a date?"

"Well, no, not exactly."

"You sure you don't want to make it a date?" she asked, resting a hand on my arm.

"Look, you're very attractive—"

"Yeah, yeah, yeah." She sat back and took a sip from her pink frothy drink.

"So anyway, I was hoping you could help me find this fellow, this Ted."

"Look, I gotta make a living—"

"I'd be glad to pay you."

The offer of money changed her attitude, and she slid her stool closer, resting her bosom against my arm. We agreed on a hundred dollars, which I thought a bit steep just for conversation, but she pointed out time was money regardless of how it was passed. I might have haggled a bit more if I'd realized how quickly my hundred was going to be spent.

"So, who is this Ted guy?" I asked.

"I don't know. I just met him a couple of weeks ago though I've seen him here a few other times. We struck up a conversation. He had to leave, and I had another date to get to, so I gave him my number. I'd sorta given up on him until I heard from you, but, of course, you're not him anyway."

"Do you know his full name or how I might reach him?"

"Hold on a second," she said, turning toward the bartender. "Hey, Frank."

It was from the bartender, and with another twenty dollars, I learned Ted dropped by for a bourbon on the rocks every Thursday after meeting with a client in Chinatown. It wasn't much to go on, but it was a Thursday. Unfortunately, Ted had already come and gone. He'd gotten to the bar just after five and was back out the door by five-thirty.

After Melissa left, I had another drink and a cigarette. I'd bought a pack of my own Camels, having exhausted the bounty found in the pocket of the coat. I promised myself I would give them up after I solved the case.

First Little Italy, now Chinatown. Were the Triads involved along with the Mafia? Was Ted some kind of bagman? And what about the bullet? Could Ted be even more nefarious, perhaps a hit man? Sitting there smoking, I wondered if I should cut my losses and stay away from Café Milan. Perhaps it was too dangerous? But I hadn't done anything wrong. Taking the coat had been an honest mistake, and I had the chance to make things right.

The following Thursday, I left work early to ensure that I would be at Café Milan well in advance of five. I hung my own coat on the rack and carried Ted's in a red and gold Macy's shopping bag to the bar. I was sitting there nursing a martini when someone tapped me on the shoulder. I turned, and there he was, tall and slim like me but wearing oversized, black-framed, thick glasses. He was a bit stooped as if he spent a lot of time at a desk. He had almost no chin, and when he spoke, it was in a hesitant whisper.

"Frank said you were looking for me. Do I know you?"

"No, not really. Trevor, Trevor Conklin," I said, offering my hand. I've never been accused of being one of those blokes who attempts to bring you to your knees with the force of his grip, but I was brought up to offer a firm handshake. Ted simply laid his hand in mine like a cold haddock. I smiled and set it aside.

He was remarkably understanding about the coat, and we had a good laugh over my foolishness. He was so happy to get it back, along with his winnings from the racetrack. He didn't even count the wad of bills.

"I have a weakness for the ponies," he confessed, "and I try to get to the race track once a month or so. When I realized that 'Sleuth' had won at Anaheim, I searched for that darn ticket everywhere. I finally suspected that I'd left it in the coat. I'm usually more careful."

"But why didn't you simply cash in the ticket?"

"Oh, the race wasn't until after three. I had to leave before then to get Ma to her hairdresser's appointment."

It turned out he lived with his mother in Scarsdale, a few stops past Bronxville. I bought Ted a bourbon on the rocks and had Frank replenish my martini.

"So, what's your line of work?" I asked.

"Accountant. I'm in business for myself and do the books for a number of small firms around town. Got an office down near Wall Street."

"Ah, so that's what brings you to Little Italy."

"Yep, there's an importer of herbal medicine a few blocks over in Chinatown. I balance his ledger once a week."

Hmm. No Triads, no Mafia. Ted wasn't turning out to be quite the character I'd imagined. I offered him another bourbon, but he refused.

"Nope, one's the limit for me. Anymore and I might end up on the bar dancing a jig."

He offered me a cigarette, and I accepted. I exhaled the smoke toward the ceiling and told him how I had tracked him down through the matchbook and the phone number. Even in the dark of the bar, I could see him blush.

"Well, actually, Melissa approached me at the bar one night," he said. "I was quite attracted to her, until the issue of money came up. Then, I realized what I was getting into. I made some excuse, but before I could leave, she wrote her number down on the matchbook. I took it, but of course, I'd never have called."

He put out his cigarette, picked up the Macy's bag holding his coat, and stood to go, thanking me for tracking him down. I apologized again for inconveniencing him. He turned for the door and then stopped and looked back.

"Excuse me, but you didn't happen to find anything else in the pocket of the coat?"

"Oh, my God, yes, the bullet." I dug into my jacket pocket and handed it to him.

"My father was a police officer," Ted explained. "He carried this bullet for luck. When he died, I started carrying it. Kind of like a rabbit's foot. Anyway, thanks." And with a wave over his shoulder, he stepped out into the night.

I took a last drag on my cigarette, chuckling to myself. I'd sure let my imagination run wild, yet the past couple of weeks had been kind of fun. More than fun, actually—exciting. Horseracing, gangsters, prostitutes, intrigue, and the big case. In a way, I regretted it was all over. Maybe I should have been a detective instead of a draftsman.

I drank the last of my martini, paid the check, and walked over to the coat rack. There next to my grey overcoat was a tan Burberry trench coat lined in plaid with all the belts, buckles, and flaps—the kind worn by foreign correspondents and spies. I slipped it on and stepped out into the street. If I rushed, I could still make the 6:28.

A Bend in the Road

My favorite moment is the union of flashing lights—the pulsing reds, the strobing blues, the spinning yellows, and searching whites from the fire trucks and ambulances, the police cars, the wreckers and tow trucks, and the passenger cars with their rubbernecking drivers. Sometimes there are even floodlights from T.V. vans lighting up the night sky, and on special occasions, a helicopter with its searchlight arcing through the dark.

Of course, the moment of the accident is always an adrenalin rush with the bursting of the guard rail, the screaming of tearing metal, the shattering of the windshield, the explosion of the gas tank, the moaning of the survivors, if any, but that jolt is almost over before it begins. No, for me, the lasting pleasure comes from the flashing lights and the attendant hustle and bustle of the aftermath. After the last accident, it took the road crew most of a week to replace the guard rail, repair the damaged culvert, shore up the embankment, and re-sod the scorched earth.

I suspect, if asked, you'd guess my favorite season is winter. With its long nights and blinding snowstorms and treacherous black ice, winter certainly has its charms, but I'm actually more a fan of autumn. Autumn, with its distracting bursts of color and slippery, wet, decaying leaves strewn across the roadway, brings just the right intimation of death in its chilly winds. Drivers can be cautious in winter but are oblivious in fall, their attention diverted by the blazing foliage.

The straightaways think I'm bent, their little joke I suppose, but I know the secret delight we all take from scenes of mayhem, as every Hollywood blockbuster proves. And what do straightaways know anyway? They are so obvious and uncomplicated, laid out flat and direct for all to see while a good bend in the road can never be taken in all at once but can only be glimpsed and understood in small, incremental moments, which as soon as they are grasped, slip from sight in the rearview mirror. It takes a real bozo, someone drunk or texting or falling asleep, to have an accident on a straightaway while even the most careful driver is at risk on a bend in the road. So I attribute the straightaways' censure to jealousy rather to any heartfelt disapproval of me. After all, we all know bends in the road don't kill drivers; drivers kill drivers.

Tonight's a perfect night. It rained earlier, and there is a fresh layer of rotting leaves on the pavement. A light fog has settled over the area. There is even a branch, blown down by the wind, obscuring the yellow caution sign warning approaching motorists of the sharp curve to the right and suggesting they slow down to twenty miles per hour.

Up ahead on the straightaway, a car has just crested the rise in the road, its headlights trying to cut through the fog as it barrels toward me. I spread my arms wide.

Spilt Milk

I t was August of 1953, the month my father started drinking, again. I was eight years old, and my heroes were Burt Lancaster, Kirk Douglas, and Alan Ladd as "Shane." But above them all was Mickey Mantle, Number 7, Center Fielder for the New York Yankees. That August, we all thought this would be the season when he'd take away Babe Ruth's record of sixty homers.

My summer days were filled with fishing for bluegills in the brown waters of the Bronx River; Saturday matinees at the RKO theater; and games of spud, pony, and ring-a-levio, played until our moms called us in for dinner. There were the two or three-day periods when we got the war bug, playing endless, complex games involving teams of marines against the Japs or the Krauts or the Commies. Then, there were the crazes: Yo-yos one week, paddle balls the next, water balloons, silly putty, chestnuts strung on shoelaces, but the one constant was baseball, which we played every summer day.

I was a lousy batter, always last in the line-up, but I was even a worse fielder, so I was put way out in right where I prayed no one would hit. The only area where I excelled was at the stats. I memorized all the scores, RBIs, and ERAs and was always called on to settle any factual dispute. But on the field, I stank, bobbling the ball and swinging late at pitches.

Truth was I didn't get much practice. While other kids spent their evenings playing catch and fielding grounders with their fathers, my dad was usually stuck at work or too tired from a long day at the office, or too busy with something really important. And the truth was he wasn't any better at baseball than I. He was more of an inside dad with his music and books and newspapers. He'd save the sports page for me, and while he read about events around the world, I'd sit nearby running my finger down the results from yesterday's games.

In those days, I always thought of myself as having two dads—the drinking dad and the dad on the wagon. The drinking dad sort of hung around on the periphery of my life, rarely appearing or showing much interest in what I was doing. But then, when I least expected it, he'd explode out of the shadows of his dark cave like a voracious, hard-shelled lobster snapping its claws. The on-the-wagon dad was more present though not necessarily more engaged. At least he was a bit more predictable and a lot more temperate. Years later when I had experience with my own drinking, I'd come to understand there was only one dad, complex and flawed, one who when drinking dreamed of being sober and when sober dreamed of drinking again.

A couple of times a year, my dad would take me to work for the day. He was in the movie business, not actually making pictures but something to do with their distribution. His office was at Rockefeller Center in the city, so we'd board the New York Central train in Yonkers and travel the half hour to Grand Central Station, with me staring out the window at the trash strewn railway bed, the desolate lots with their abandoned cars, the rusted hoppers idling on forgotten sidings... and my father reading the Saturday Evening Post.

On those days, I'd wear a white shirt and a red knit tie. My father dressed in a dark blue suit of which he had six—one for each day of the week and one for the cleaners. He was tall and slim, and now, when I look at photos from those days, I can see he was handsome, even elegant, his wavy, brown hair short on the top and long on the sides and swept back the way the English often look.

As we'd approach Manhattan, we'd cross the river and ride the elevated track over the streets of Harlem, rushing along between the grimy, brick tenements with their sooty windows open to catch the fleeting morning breeze. I'd press my nose to the train's window, hoping to get a glimpse of the foreign lives lurking behind the fluttering curtains. Sometimes I'd catch a glimpse of an ebony-skinned woman wearing only a slip, leaning out her window staring back at the passing railway cars.

Before heading downtown to Grand Central Station, the train made one stop at 125th Street. Only a few of the white, male riders would disembark, but a number of Negroes, as I was instructed to say back then, mostly women in plain cloth dresses, got on and huddled near the doorway for the ride downtown. On this day, two men sat on the platform with their backs propped up against a green billboard advertising Kool cigarettes. One of the men was sleeping, and his trousers were wet. The other held a bottle in a brown bag and looked up at me. As the train lurched forward, he raised the bottle and nodding, tipped it toward me before taking a drink. I turned my eyes to the floor of the railway car and kept them there until we plunged into the darkness of the tunnels running under the streets of New York.

For lunch on our days in the city, my father took me to the Rainbow Room on the 65th Floor of Rockefeller Center with its magnificent view of the skyline. As usual, I asked for the shrimp cocktail, a hamburger, and a chocolate milk. My father ordered the lobster. Every time he ate a lobster, he'd explain the proper way to open it so as not to ruin the meat. He'd wave the monstrous red claw at me and then crack the shell removing the meat whole. He'd dip the flesh in butter and pop it into his mouth.

He'd snap his jaws, swallow and grin, and say, "See?" a thin line of butter usually running down his chin, which he'd dab with his crisp, white napkin.

Two of his friends from the office had joined us for lunch, Mr. Small and Mrs. Feldman. Mostly, the grown-ups talked among themselves while I sipped my milk. Mr. Small and Mrs. Feldman drank martinis. My dad drank a Coke with lemon. My dad had been on the wagon since Christmas when he'd passed out at the table, and my mother had to pull his face out of the mashed potatoes and gravy before he drowned.

As I was finishing my shrimp cocktail, I looked around the room; the crystal goblets and heavy silverware laid out on the creased tablecloths sparkled in the afternoon light. Over in the corner, a man looked up from his plate. He winked at me and tilted back his glass and drained the last of its amber liquid. He turned to a waiter and shook his glass for a refill. He leaned over to the guy sitting next to him and said something that made the other laugh. The guy laughing was Whitey Ford, the star pitcher of the Yankees whose 18-6 win-loss record would be an important factor in the Yankees getting to the World Series that year. The man who had winked at me was Mickey Mantle.

"Dad?"

"I'm talking to Mr. Small. You know better than to interrupt."

"But Dad…."

"That's alright, Fred," said Mr. Small. "What's up, Tommy?"

I looked at my dad.

"Okay, son. What's so important?"

"The man over in the corner. That's Mickey Mantle."

My father, Mr. Small, and Mrs. Feldman turned to look over at the corner table.

"I think the boy's right," said Mr. Small.

"Well, that's great," said my dad. "You'll have something to tell your friends about tomorrow."

"But Dad, Mickey winked at me."

"Aren't you lucky," said Mrs. Feldman, sipping from her cocktail. "I hear he usually only winks at the ladies."

For some reason, the grown-ups thought this was funny.

"We need to get his autograph."

"Oh, I don't think so, Tommy. Mr. Mantle doesn't want to be bothered while he's having his lunch. People don't ask for autographs in a place like this."

"But Dad, no one will believe me. No one will believe I saw him and that he winked at me unless I get his autograph. I've got to get it."

"They'll believe you. I'll tell them I saw him, too."

"I wonder what they've done with our entrees," said Mr. Small, craning his neck to the left and the right. "I've got a two o'clock downtown."

"Dad?"

"Tommy, that's enough. Stop interrupting. We're not going to bother Mr. Mantle about a silly autograph."

For the next half hour, I nibbled on my burger and pushed ketchup around my plate with the French fries. I kept looking over to the corner, but Mickey didn't look my way again. The grown-ups paid the bill, and while they were waiting for their change, I tried one last time.

Pulling on my father's suit sleeve, I said, "Please."

"Tommy—"

"Remember you said you saw Babe Ruth play one time at Yankee Stadium. He hit a homer and drove in Lou Gehrig, and they won the game. Remember? Don't you wish you had his autograph? Don't you?"

My father looked at me for a moment. "Come on."

He put his hand on my shoulder and walked me across the room to Mickey Mantle's table. Whitey saw us first and nodded his head our way. Mickey looked up and frowned. Then he saw me and said something I couldn't hear to Whitey and seemed to settle back in his chair. He reached forward and took a sip of his coffee, putting the cup back in its saucer as we stepped up to the table.

"Sorry to bother you Mr. Mantle, but the boy—"

"No sweat," Mickey said, offering his hand to my dad. My father reached across the table to shake Mickey's hand, and as he did so, he turned and nodded toward Whitey. Halfway across the table, my father's pinky finger went through the loop of the handle on the cream pitcher, lifting it airborne and sailing it across the table where it landed in Mickey's lap, splattering cream down the front of his suit.

"Goddamn it!" Mickey yelled, rising from his chair. His fists were clenched, and his face had turned a blistering red. He reached across the table with his left hand, trying to grab my father's shirtfront while cocking his right fist back. Whitey grabbed Mickey by the waist and pulled him back into his seat.

"No, Mick. They'll sue your ass. Don't do it."

"Sorry, sorry," my father mumbled, backing away from the table, his head bowed, his shoulders slumped. I followed, taking furtive glances back at the chaos surrounding Mickey's table as several waiters elbowed each other aside to dab linen napkins at his suit and shirt.

My father stopped by his office just long enough to tell his secretary he would be taking the rest of the afternoon off. By three o'clock, we were seated side-by-side on worn, wooden stools hidden in the dark recesses of the Oyster Bar at Grand

Central Station. The lobster tanks bubbled nearby, their lights casting a speckled pattern on the bar's bleak walls. I looked up and saw our reflections in the back-bar mirror through row upon row of half-filled green, brown, and clear bottles. My father was smoking Chesterfields and drinking scotch. I was drinking chocolate milk and munching on oyster crackers.

As my father signaled the bartender for another round, I said, "I think I've had enough chocolate milk for the day. Maybe we should call it quits."

My father turned his head to look at me as the bartender set down another scotch. He lit a new cigarette off the smoldering butt of his old one. He took a drag and started to speak. "You see, Tommy, there's this hole...."

He went silent for a moment before continuing. "Never mind. Maybe someday you'll understand."

He turned again to look at the mirror and the rows of half-empty bottles. In the quiet, I heard the buzz of a refrigerator, the gurgle of the lobster tank, the clink of ice as my father twirled his drink, and, in the distance, the hustle of the crowds rushing to meet their trains.

The Creek

The evening before the day my sister watched me nearly die, my father was drunk, as usual, and raving about what shits people were. Growing up, we spent every July at The Hut on Long Island's Southold Bay. The summer of 1953 was no different.

That evening, my father's audience was Mr. Small, an insurance agent from Yonkers, and Mr. Segal, who ran a furniture store over in Mt. Vernon, friends who had joined us for the weekend. An Irish Catholic, a Jew, and my father, a fallen Scottish Presbyterian, the three of them bound together in a communion of gin, well fueled to settle the issue of the nature of man.

"Shits, I tell you," my father proclaimed, pointing his finger to the heavens. "Always looking out for themselves. Steal you blind if given half a chance. You can't trust anyone." My father had recently been bilked out of some money in a scam my mother told me I was too young to understand, and he was not parting with his anger gracefully.

"You're so full of shite; I'm surprised I can see the whites of your eyes," said Mr. Small, his florid face even redder from the gin and an afternoon of fishing. "How are we supposed to survive as a species without trust? If there's a problem, it's that people have moved away from the church. All men are sinners, 'tis true," Mr. Small continued, "but through the love of Christ, they can learn to trust and love their fellow man."

My father narrowed his eyes. There'd been some recent trouble at Mr. Small's firm with the tax people, and my father was raising his finger again, perhaps to bring this up, when Mr. Segal broke in.

"The Talmud teaches us man was formed with two impulses: a good impulse and an evil one." He took a sip from his now watery martini. "Man has both a moral conscience, an inner voice if you will, that reminds him of God's commandments when he's tempted to do something wrong and a desire to satisfy his personal wants without regard for the consequences to others. Of course, we need to have a desire to fulfill our needs, or we wouldn't get anything done, but if left unchecked, it can lead to misbehavior. So, you see, there is an implicit tension in being human."

My father and Mr. Small stared at Mr. Segal, each taking a long pull from their drinks.

"Steal you blind."

"But with the love of Christ...."

I left them and walked into the house, entering the kitchen. My mother and Mrs. Small and Mrs. Segal leaned against the counters holding sweating glasses of gin and tonic, cigarettes balanced between the fingers of their free hands. My mother looked over at me standing in the door. "Are the men alright?"

I shrugged my shoulders. "I don't know. They're talking about Jesus and shit."

"Don't you dare use that word in this house," my mother said, as Mrs. Small snorted gin out through her nose.

"What's wrong with saying 'Jesus?'"

"Don't be smart with me. You know exactly what I mean. Now, give me a hug. It's time for your bed."

As I climbed the creaking wooden stairs to my room, I heard laughter from the kitchen and from the porch, my father and Mr.

Small breaking into a rendition of "My Darling Clementine,"—that July's theme song.

As I stepped out on the porch the following morning, my father turned from gazing at the pink horizon, a steaming cup of coffee resting on the railing, a Chesterfield smoldering in his hand. Back in Yonkers, our fourth-floor apartment offered only a modest view of a paved courtyard with two towering oaks and an identical apartment building across the way. On vacation, no matter how much he'd had to drink the night before, my father made a point of waking in time to see the sunrise. To the east, the creek meandered in front of The Hut before making a final turn and emptying into Southold Bay. Due to its proximity to the open sea, the creek was affected by the tides and would reverse its course as the tide rose, carrying the brackish seawater back past The Hut and upstream into Hashamomuck Pond. Then, the creek would become still, waiting for the pull of the moon and sun to empty again into the bay. That morning, the water was flowing to the sea; ripples catching the light of the dawn threw sparks into the air.

"Morning, Son."

I rubbed my eyes and looked toward the sun as it crested the sandy bank separating the creek from the bay beyond.

"A beautiful day," he said, nodding toward the sunrise and sipping from his cup.

"Even with all the shits you can't trust?" I asked, the image of my sister in my mind.

My father frowned then smiled. "Ah, yes."

He took a drag from his cigarette and exhaled the smoke into the morning breeze. "Yeah, there are a lot of unpleasant characters around, but the surprising thing is every now and then, someone will unexpectedly do something generous, be there for you when you don't expect it. Folks will surprise you. You'll find people you can rely on, someone you can trust. You keep your eyes peeled." He flicked the smoldering butt out on to the lawn, and as it hissed in the dew, he turned away from me to watch the sun draped in purple clouds break free from the horizon and begin its long climb into the sky.

In the late afternoon, my mother announced, "The grown-ups are going for a drive. We need to pick up a few things in town, and we might head over to Greenport to see if the lobster boat is in. We shouldn't be more than a couple of hours, three at tops." My sister smiled. I knew she had hopes for that afternoon.

"Anne, you keep an eye on your brother," Mom added. My sister shot me a flinty look, curling back her lip.

My sister was five years older and as bossy and mean as any thirteen-year-old sister could be. I had the bruises to prove it. If she wasn't wailing away on me, she'd be explaining how I was adopted, or retarded, or had some secret disease that no one would talk about but which would kill me before too long. She confided how my parents didn't love me; they just pitied me. I wasn't without blame for our difficult relationship. I messed with her stuff at every opportunity and tattled to our parents when I could appear to be concerned rather than simply squealing.

That summer, my sister was working on a boyfriend. Junior, or Junie as everyone called him, was the son of Mr. Grayson, the manager of the potato farm on which we rented The Hut. Junie was fourteen and strong, swift, and sure. He was friendly enough to me, but even then, I realized his kindness was tied to his interest in my sister. And my sister could attract interest. She was tall and blond, and already she had a woman's figure. Even I could see she was beautiful.

The six adults clambered into Mr. Small's red and white DeSoto and sped off down the dirt lane, tires skidding, gravel pinging against the undercarriage, a brown cloud of dust trailing behind them. I dealt my deck of cards to play solitaire. Soon after the grown-ups left, Junie ambled down the lane and crossed over to our porch. Anne and Junie walked a little away and sat on the lawn, their backs to me, their heads bent together. They talked too quietly for me to hear, and then my sister stood. "We're just going to take a walk down to the creek."

"I want to go."

"No. You have to stay here. We won't be long."

"No. Mom said you have to watch me. I'll tell."

My sister clenched a fist and took a step toward me.

"Aw, it's okay," said Junie. "Let him come along. It doesn't matter."

Anne glanced at Junie with a puzzled look that seemed to say, 'Is this the best I can do?' Then, she shook her head and stepped on to the sandy path that led to the creek. Junie followed with me close behind.

When she reached the narrow beach at the edge of the creek, my sister sat down on the sand, picked up a handful of pebbles and shells, and flipped them one-by-one into the water. Junie sat down beside her, and I waded into the gentle current up to my knees and dug my toes into the sandy bottom hoping to dislodge a clam. As I hadn't learned to swim yet, I was only allowed to go this far into the water unless I was with my father. I squinted my eyes against the mid-day glare of the sun bouncing off the creek's shifting surface.

The water in the creek was brown, filled with leaves and twigs and the tannins it collected passing through woods and marshes on its journey to the bay. In its deeper parts, the water looked black, the bottom impossible to see. When the tide rose

161

and the creek reversed course and flowed backward, it was easy to swim or paddle a canoe up to the bend a mile or so upstream where the farm's property ended. If you timed it just right, you could float up the creek, wait a bit sitting on the bank at the bend, and then ride the flow back down again as the tide went out. I'd often taken this trip with my father in our canoe. When we'd get to the bend to wait, my father would open a small cooler, and we'd share a peanut butter or egg salad sandwich while I drank a coke and he a beer or two.

So it wasn't completely unreasonable when Junie said, "The tide's about in. Why don't we swim up the creek and wait for it to turn? Then we can float back down?"

"I can't," my sister said, giving a nod in my direction.

"Why not?"

"You know he can't swim."

"Shoot, he doesn't weigh anything. I can carry him on my back."

"I can dog paddle," I said.

"Yeah, for a couple of feet."

"Come on. It'll be fun. He can just grab on to my shoulders."

My sister hesitated, looking first at me then at the water, "I don't know…." But Junie was already heading for the water's edge. She turned to me. "Okay, but no fooling around. You hold on tight to Junie."

My sister rose from the hot sand and walked into the creek. When the water reached her thighs, she dived toward the center of the stream, disappearing for a moment before rising, tilting her face back and dipping her head once more so her blond hair sluiced off her face. Junie followed her, slicing through the water's surface like an arrow. He rose just inches from my sister.

"Hey, what about me?" I yelled.

162

Junie turned and smiled and with four or five strong strokes swam back to where I stood, the creek's current slipping around my knees.

"Hop aboard," he said, kneeling down in the water so I could reach his shoulders.

With my arms around his neck, he pushed off. He reached up and tugged at my hands to loosen them a bit from his throat. As we moved off into the center of the stream, I could feel his feet bouncing along the creek's bottom. With a kick, we were launched and moving upstream, gently propelled by the lift of the rising tide.

For the first minute or two, we seemed to be doing fine. Junie would take a breath of air then let his face sink beneath the surface as I raised my head to keep my mouth above the water line. Soon though, his breaths turned to gasps. I tightened my grip as he struggled to get his head above water. My sister swimming along the side of us yelled, "Head for the shore."

But Junie, now flailing, veered the opposite way into even deeper water. Gulping and gasping, he threw me from his back. "He's too heavy; I can't carry him."

I suppose I tried dog paddling but to no avail. It was quiet and the light dim in the dark water. Though I must have been frantic, what I remember after all these years is a calm and a peace. That calm and peace may have been real or it may be an invention constructed through the filter of time, but what followed is as clear as yesterday.

A hand grabbed my arm and pulled me up. My sister. I thrashed at her, clawing at her shoulders and her face. She yelled for me to stop and to relax, but I screamed and wrapped my arms around her head pushing her under. She struggled to the surface one more time, her legs scissoring frantically. She went under again, pulling me down with her. Then I felt a thump through her body as her foot struck the bottom of the creek. And then another and another, and we hopped our way into the shallows and crawled up the bank.

We sprawled among the ferns and weeds, me crying, her coughing. When our breathing settled, I raised my head and saw Junie racing across a pasture to his house. I lowered my head again and turned on my side facing my sister. A tear traced down her cheek, or perhaps, it was just water running from her hair and into her eyes.

"You can't tell," she said.

"I won't."

She looked at me then shook her head. "You'll tell."

"No, I won't. You can trust me." And it was true, she could, but even as I said it, I realized it was I who could trust her.

She ditched me the next day to sneak off with Junie. Over the weeks and months and years that followed, I still tormented her, messing with her things and invading her privacy, and she still tortured me, the bruises and the indignities continuing. Even as adults, we argued and hurt each other, knowing precisely the buttons to push, even once going several months without speaking. Yet after that afternoon in the summer of 1953, there was no time when trust and truth were needed when we couldn't turn to each other. Even today, ten years after her death, I'll think for a split second, I need to call Anne about that before I remember there is no more calling Anne, and I'll think back to the day when my father instructed me to keep my eyes open for trust, and I found it.

Pothole

T he pothole waits in the road at the corner of Coliseum and Lyon in the Uptown neighborhood of New Orleans. It is small. It has been small before, and it will be small again, but sometimes it is large: big enough to swallow a Winn-Dixie shopping cart or a baby stroller or the front end of a United Taxi. After the hole begins to devour these various conveyances, the men in jumpsuits arrive with their backhoes and dig at the hole. They fix the pipe, or so they think, and fill the hole with sand and gravel and pour hot asphalt on the hole and roll the black macadam with heavy machines. But the hole is patient. It can sense the water still seeping from the rusted cast iron pipe below, eroding the sand and gravel and flushing away the cigarette butts and the discarded wrappers from the Rally's burgers the work crew left behind. First the hole eats its way under the asphalt causing a mild depression. It can feel the cars jolting as they pass overhead. Then one day a small chunk of the pavement gives way and falls inward, and noon sunlight enters the hole and warms and softens the earth below. A neighbor places a flag or a traffic cone or a trash can over the hole to warn off passing motorists. Once a beautiful woman placed a potted palm tree over the hole, but a student from Tulane stole it in a matter of minutes. The hole feels the rumble of trucks from above, loosening the joints of the water pipe, and the water flows faster. The hole has been growing quietly below the street. The black surface is further undermined and about to give way. The hole hears the newspaper delivery truck approaching, and it widens its maw.

The Wolf Man

More than forty years have passed since Maddie suggested we shit-bag Witch Hazel's house on Halloween night. To be fair, when I think back on that night in 1956, I don't remember Billy or I offering much resistance.

"She wants to do what?" I'd asked.

"Shit-bag. You know," Billy said, "you get a paper bag of dog shit, soak it in lighter fluid, put it on someone's door stoop, light it, and ring their bell. Then you watch them stomp it out."

At the time, the three of us were in Mrs. Slocomb's sixth grade class at P.S. 30. Hazel Slocomb or, as we called her, Witch Hazel was a fixture at our Yonkers elementary school. Her hair was gray, and her face wrinkled and ashen. We thought she must have been a hundred years old. She had a habit of drinking cup after cup of black coffee out of an old, red plaid thermos. Each time she unscrewed the stopper, we knew by the pungent fumes she was pouring more than just coffee. And she could be incredibly cruel, growing more horrible as the day dragged on, especially toward Billy.

"Who turned in this moronic essay? Oh, Billy Kohler. Big surprise there."

"Yes. Billy, I saw your hand. If I had wanted an incorrect answer from an idiot, I certainly would have called on you."

As the hours crept by, Billy seemed to shrink, slinking lower and lower behind his desk.

So no, neither of us argued when Maddie said, "Look, this is going to be our last Halloween. You don't see junior high kids out tonight. Witch Hazel's been riding Billy since the first day of school. What better night to get even?"

Back then, the Million Dollar Movie showed films on Channel 9 from the thirties and forties. Each week, they played one movie over and over again, twice each night. For the run-up to Halloween, they screened old horror films. My parents disapproved of scary movies, so a couple of weeks before Halloween on a Saturday evening, I headed over to Billy's where the rules were slacker.

I pedaled my Schwinn through our small corner of Yonkers, passing the Rexall's where my father worked and Augie's where we idled after school over Cokes and egg creams. The storefronts were draped in orange and black, and silhouettes of witches and goblins hung in the windows. I rode over the bridge spanning the train tracks that ran south to New York City. At Billy's, I climbed the outside metal staircase, its black paint flaking, the rusted steps groaning with every footfall.

On nights when I slept over, Mrs. Kohler slept in Billy's small bedroom, and we took her foldout couch in the living room next to the Sylvania. Billy's mother, exhausted from her job at Mac and Ann's Diner, was in bed long before us. There wasn't any Mr. Kohler.

"This is going to scare the piss out of you, Larry. You gotta promise not to wet the bed."

"I'm not going to wet the bed. What's it called again?"

"Frankenstein. Boris Karloff plays the monster. Frankenstein's this crazy scientist."

We kept the volume low and leaned in close to the flickering screen. The picture was grainy no matter how much we fiddled with the aluminum foil taped to the rabbit ears. Soon the lousy reception no longer mattered as we became lost in the German countryside, being chased by the monster and angry villagers.

"Scary, huh?"

"I guess, but I feel sorta sorry for Frankenstein…. I mean the monster. He didn't really mean to hurt anyone."

"Don't be such a wimp. Believe me, if the monster ever got a hold of you, he'd rip your arms clean off."

We spent the next week perfecting our stiff-armed, staggering walks. "Aaargh." "Friend." "Aaargh." We decided to try out our Frankensteins on Maddie, who lived next door to Billy. She was by far the prettiest girl in our school. Billy once asked her to go to the movies, but she said her dad wouldn't let her. I'd danced with her a couple of times at school dances, my palms sweating from fear she'd notice my erection, but she didn't seem to, as she pushed against me so close one of the chaperones tapped us on the shoulder and wiggled her hand between us.

When we tried out our monster moves on Maddie, she laughed. "You guys look like constipated robots."

"You don't know what you're talking about. Frankenstein's cool," said Billy, lurching around the yard. I looked at Maddie and back at Billy, and I could see what she meant.

"Just wait," she said, "next week they're showing Dracula."

While I sympathized with the dimwitted Frankenstein monster, Dracula and his spooky brides evoked nothing but terror. Billy and I spent fifty cents each at Woolworth's for a few feet of black cloth, and we fashioned capes by tying the ends around our necks. With globs of Vaseline, we slicked back our unruly hair. We practiced a Transylvanian accent until we were convinced we'd nailed it.

Approaching Maddie, I covered my face with the black cape so that only my eyes showed. I slunk toward her saying, "I vant to suck your blood." Instead of laughing, she tilted her head to the right. I hesitated a second before leaning in. One of the straps of the bra she had begun to wear that year peeked out from the sleeve of her dress. I smelled lilac and tasted something salty as I brushed my lips against her neck. Though I understood the horror of Dracula, at least the type of fear he held for a twelve-year-old boy, I'd still to learn the true meaning of his seductive power. But Maddie knew.

"No, this is how you do it."

She rested her lips against my neck, her teeth brushing my skin, her breath warm and wet. Then she bit down hard. I shoved her away.

"What, are you crazy?" I yelled, rubbing the tender spot.

Maddie, an unpleasant gleam in her eyes, turned and walked back into her house.

It wasn't the first time she'd done something cruel and unexpected. I had a scar on my shoulder from where she'd dropped a sparkler down my shirt at a Fourth of July picnic. And I wasn't the only one. A number of kids at school had been hurt by Maddie's pranks, yet no matter how many times Maddie was mean, after a bit of sulking, I'd find myself returning to her, as to a mosquito bite you can't stop scratching no matter how much it bleeds.

"Dracula's stupid," said Billy, taking off his cape and stomping off to leave me standing in the yard alone.

A few nights before Halloween, the Million Dollar Movie showed The Wolf Man. For me, the Wolf Man was the perfect monster, a regular guy, not some creature made from body parts or a bloodsucker who rose from the dead. His name was Larry

Talbot in the movie. Larry, the same as me, not a weird name like Dracula or Frankenstein. And the fact a wolf had bitten Larry seemed plausible. Half the kids in my class had been bitten by dogs, treated with a swab of iodine and a caution not to pet strange animals. For a twelve-year-old kid, it was a small step to werewolves and full moons.

As sixth graders, we were too old to go trick-or-treating on Halloween, but we weren't too old to dress up and roam the streets looking for mischief and a chance to take revenge on Witch Hazel. Choosing our costumes was easy. With green face paint and my father's work boots, Billy turned into Frankenstein's monster. With a generous application of talcum powder and her mother's red lipstick and wearing a long black dress, Maddie became the Bride of Dracula. I bought a black wig designed for a Pocahontas costume and some snaggle teeth. I cut out eyeholes and a gap for the mouth and tied the wig over my face with the jagged teeth sticking through. I took my rabbit fur-lined gloves and turned them inside out for paws. I was the perfect Wolf Man.

If the moon wasn't full, it was close enough, rising clear and bright over our neighborhood, the limbs of the barren trees casting spindly shadows across our path. There was a chill to the night, and the smoky scent of burning leaves drifted in the air. We jumped out of bushes, scaring some of the younger kids and making them hand over a candy bar or two.

We'd already TP'd Crazy Caruthers's house when Billy turned to me. "I dare you to go up on the Taylors' porch and peek through the window."

"That's stupid."

"Chicken," Billy said, clucking and flapping his arms and strutting around in a circle. I looked at Maddie for support, but she was watching Billy and smiling.

I crept along the hedgerow to the Taylors' house, crawled up the splintery steps of their porch, and crouched down below their living room window. I raised my head. Mrs. Taylor sat in a pink dress, her feet, in fuzzy yellow slippers, resting on a dark leather ottoman. She was watching The Mummy, a movie I'd not yet seen. As the Mummy crept across the screen, dragging one foot behind him and with bits of bandage and skin peeling away, I heard a footfall.

Mr. Taylor let out a high-pitched yell when I turned around, and he saw my hairy face and protruding teeth. I spied the baseball bat grasped in his hands and dove over the porch railing as he took a swing at me. I ran off into the darkness, Mr. Taylor's screams and curses chasing me into the night.

"Man, that was something," I said, my heart racing. "Did you see Old Man Taylor? Did you see the bat? Jesus, that was close."

"Yeah, terrific," said Billy.

"Terrific? That's all I get after nearly getting killed."

"Don't mind Billy. He's just having a little chicken moment of his own," said Maddie.

"What?"

"She wants to shit-bag Slocomb's house."

"Shit-bag? Is that real?"

"Ask her."

Maddie looked at us as if measuring our worth. She shook her head. "Maybe you guys are just too scared."

Locating dog waste wasn't a problem in those days, but finding lighter fluid was. My parents smoked but just used matches. Billy solved the problem by dipping his handkerchief into the gas tank of a motorcycle parked a block from Slocomb's.

With the moon high in the sky, we approached her house, dark except for the flickering glow coming from a TV in her living room. Maddie and I hid in the bushes across the street. Billy crept up the stairs of her porch. He set the sodden bag down on her brown, hemp doormat and struck a match. He pitched the match toward the bag, and with a whoosh even we could hear, it burst into flames. Billy leaned on the doorbell before dashing across the street to join us in our lair.

The front door flew open, and there stood Witch Hazel, dressed in a long, black nightgown, her gray hair falling wildly about her shoulders. A cigarette dangled from her lips, and a glass of brown liquid sloshed in her left hand. The welcome mat was on fire; the gasoline fed flames reaching three feet high.

With a screech, she dumped the brown liquid on the fire, but the alcohol only fueled its anger. She leapt on to the blaze, swirling like a deranged dervish, trying to stomp out the flames. Burning globs of dog feces splattered the porch, the wicker furniture, and Slocomb's nightgown. As the flames caught hold of the fabric, she froze for one moment, her gaze, searching through the dark, rested on the bushes where we hid. As the blaze engulfed her, she shrieked into the night, a sound more like a curse than a cry. Arms flailing, she stumbled back into the house, the pitiful yelps of her agony carrying across the street to where we crouched.

"Oh, Christ," I said.

Billy just sat there, shaking his head, a dangle of spit leaking from his mouth.

Maddie gazed at the fire, its light dancing in her eyes.

"Oh, Christ," I said again.

Even though the house was old and made of wood and our autumn had been dry, it still seems improbable to me how in minutes, the flames spread to the curtains and engulfed the living room. They leapt to the second story, breaking through the roof. Neighbors gathered, standing futilely holding rakes and hoes and axes; kids, still costumed as hobos, princesses, and pirates, looked on with mouths open and eyes squinting against the brightness. Sirens wailed in the distance.

We slunk back to an alley on our side of the street and ran off. At its end, we paused out of breath, bathed in the pale moonlight breaking through the bare, spindly branches overhead.

Maddie spoke first. "Not a word. Never. Swear," and put out her hand.

Billy rested his hand on hers, nodding. "I swear."

Maddie looked at me, "Swear."

"Jesus, Maddie. Jesus."

"Swear."

"Billy, we—"

"No, Larry, you gotta swear."

I stood staring back into his eyes for a moment before taking off my furry glove and placing my hand on top of his and Maddie's. "I swear."

The morning's Herald Statesman reported that while the fire department had arrived in time to save the neighboring houses, Mrs. Slocomb's home was reduced to ashes. The cause of the fire was unknown; however, it was suspected that Mrs. Slocomb, a known smoker, had nodded off while watching TV, a smoldering cigarette causing the blaze.

The paper ran a picture of Mrs. Slocomb in an Army nurse's uniform from World War I. The article said she was highly decorated and credited with bravery and saving many lives in field hospitals in France. She'd met her husband, a pilot, while they were both on leave in England. The Germans shot him down on one of the last missions of the war. She quit nursing to become a teacher. She had no known relatives though one neighbor thought she'd heard of a son out in California, but she'd never seen him. Mrs. Slocomb was sixty-one.

The next fall we entered Lincoln Junior and Senior High School, and there was no talk of going out on Halloween. As the year marched on, we drifted apart.

Maddie started wearing make-up and riding around town with high school boys in late model Pontiacs and Buicks.

Billy took to slicking back his hair like Elvis and to wearing his collar turned up. He hung out with a gang of eighth and ninth graders, smoking and drinking beer down by the Bronx River. At the end of the year, he and his mother moved out of state.

During those junior high years, a new rash of monster movies appeared. Some were remakes: a new *Frankenstein* and *Dracula*, and even a movie about a teenage werewolf. There were new monsters, too: creatures haunting black lagoons, giant lizards and moths destroying Japan, beasts slithering under the sea, and giant ants roaming the sewers of Los Angeles. I saw none of them.

By then, I was more concerned with the human monsters walking among us. I knew there were ones made from bits and pieces of insults and injustices handed out by vengeful teachers and absent fathers. Others formed in a cauldron of life's misfortunes. I knew some monsters were born whole with no other explanation than that's the way they were. And I knew there was a fourth type of monster, the accidental one who meets his fate on an unfortunate night under an unforgiving moon.

I still live in Yonkers. Augie's is long gone, but the Rexall's remains, now owned by CVS. I teach sixth grade at the elementary school, not at the long-shuttered P.S. 30 but at the new school on Mt. Vernon Avenue. Last week on Halloween, avoiding the street where Mrs. Slocomb's house once stood, I accompanied my daughter in her Pocahontas costume, protecting her for another year from the swarms of ghouls, witches, vampires, and werewolves stalking the moonlit night.

Some of the stories in this collection were published in the following:

The Berkshire Review: "The Lady in the Window."
The Briar Cliff Review: "Muskrats."
CHA: An Asian Literary Journal: "A Night at the Taj."
Delmarva Review: "The Guildemeister" and "The Flight."
Louisiana: In Words: "The Pothole (published as 4:23.)"
The Literary Lunch Room: "Salt."
Oracle: "The Story Teller."
Seven Hills Review: "The Guy in the Box," "A New York Moment," "The Bend in the Road," "The Man with No Nose," "The One-Upper," "Ash Wednesday," "The Lakeview Motel," The Wolf Man," and "Sisters."
The Timber Creek Review: "Poaching."

.

Author's Note

Many of these stories benefited from the contributions of the members of the Loyola Writers' Group in New Orleans and the Broadneck Writers' Group in Annapolis. Over the years, James Nolan, Laura Oliver, Lynn Schwartz, and Charles Wilkinson provided me with valued advice on most of the stories included in this collection. For her constant support and inspired insights in the writing of these stories, I thank my wife, Ann